Missing in Australia

An Anna Davies Mystery

Book 5

Rita Lee Chapman

Also by Rita Lee Chapman

Anna Davies Mystery Series

Winston – A Horse's Tale

Dangerous Associations

The Poinciana Tree

For family and friends,
for what is life without them?

Contents

Part One

Chapter One
"Surprise!"

"Anna, darling, I'm taking you out for dinner tonight!" Mike called out, as he came through the front door, a big smile on his face.

"That would be nice. What's made you so excited?"

"My new contract! I've booked a table at our favourite Italian restaurant for seven o'clock."

"What new contract?"

"I'll tell you over dinner. Wear something glamorous – you're going to love this! We'll celebrate with champagne!"

Two hours later we were sitting at our favourite table, overlooking the water. I had worn my little black dress, which fitted in all the right places, with black high heels. Mike had given me a wolf whistle when I had walked into the loungeroom.

The waiter opened the champagne Mike had ordered with a flourish.

"Here's to us!" Mike toasted, as soon as it was poured.

"Well, come on, tell me; it's not fair to keep me

1

guessing. Where are we headed to this time?"

Mike smiled knowingly and paused until the waiter had left. He was an IT consultant and his work had taken him to places as exciting as Dubai and France.

"You know it can only be one of two places! I did promise you on the plane coming home from France that I would only take a contract in London – or Australia. As long as you promised to give up investigating mysteries wherever we go!" His blue eyes met mine as he said it and I was reminded how much my promise meant to him.

I nodded. I had agreed not to become involved again and I had meant it. My last little foray had nearly cost me my life and I wasn't keen to take that chance again. I had also been torn by the result, which had caused a lot of pain for all parties.

"So, don't keep me in suspense," I remonstrated with him, as we savoured the bubbles. "Are we staying here or are we off to Australia?"

"Australia!"

"Hurray!" I exclaimed. "That's wonderful." I felt a surge of joy at the thought of going back to the country where I was born, even it if was only for a short time.

We clinked our glasses and sipped some more

champagne.

"How long is it for?"

"A year. I thought that was perfect. It will give you some time back in Australia but we won't be away for too long. After all, we've only been back in London for four months."

"I know. It seems less than that, actually. How long before we leave?"

Mike cleared his throat. "Ah, well, that's the thing." He paused, to give me a chance to be prepared. "They want me to start in two weeks."

He looked at me, anxiously, wanting to know if I was okay with this. We had barely settled back into our house in London. Not only that, but his sons, Simon and James, had not seen much of us over the last couple of years because we had been in France. Our grandson, Thomas, who had recently turned two, was starting to feel comfortable with us. It was going to be a big wrench to leave them again.

"I know how much you miss Australia, Anna. I thought you'd be pleased."

"I am, Mike, I'm thrilled. It's such a surprise, that's all. It will be wonderful."

"You'll be able to catch up with Sandra and David. I

3

know how disappointed you were that they couldn't make it over to France to see us. Now you'll have the chance to spend time with Sandra."

Sandra is my best friend, who lives in Australia. We haven't seen much of each other over the last few years.

I gave him my warmest smile. "I can't wait! It is a lovely surprise and I am excited. Which city in Australia?"

"Sydney, of course! I wouldn't have taken anything in Darwin or Perth. I know you wouldn't want to be that far from Sandra and where you used to live."

"Thank you, Mike, that's great news. It will be nice to be back there - even if it's only for a year," I added, pointedly.

"I think I'll have to go on ahead and leave you to sort things out this end. You can join me whenever you are ready," Mike said, totally ignoring my comment.

"Yes, that's a good idea. With the best will in the world, I don't think I can be ready in two weeks."

We broke off to look at the menu. I found it hard to concentrate on food when so many things were whirling around in my mind. I ordered my usual, veal scallopini. Mike opted for the Italian chicken.

"Are we going to try to rent the house again?" I asked,

as the waiter finished taking our order.

"What do you think?"

"I guess we might as well. It's probably better to have someone living in it."

"We can lock our personal things away in the back bedroom, like we did last time. You wouldn't have to wait for a tenant to be found before you join me; we can put it in the hands of the same real estate agent and let them get on with it."

"I suppose." I thought for a moment or two. "I don't think we'll have any trouble renting it, with demand so high at the moment."

My veal was delicious and Mike was enjoying his chicken dish.

"What do you think James and Simon are going to say about us disappearing again - especially to the other side of the world?" I asked as we studied the dessert menu.

Mike shrugged. "They're busy with their own lives. They'd do the same if they were in my position. Besides, you know I'm planning on early retirement – we'll have plenty of time to spend with them then!"

We both ordered the tiramisu and finished the last of the champagne, deciding to have coffee at home. Once there, Mike poured us both a Baileys liqueur, whilst I made the coffee. Then we settled down on the sofa and talked about Sydney. I found myself becoming more and more excited at the thought of spending time back there. However, despite the champagne and two glasses of Baileys, sleep evaded me that night; I was too busy planning and organising in my head. First thing in the morning, I would start writing a list of things to do.

Chapter Two
Australia – Here I Come!

Twelve days later, I drove Mike to the airport. He had offered to take the train, a quick and easy alternative, but with his case taking up the full baggage allowance, his cabin bag and laptop, I couldn't let him struggle on the train. I kissed him goodbye at the airport and told him I would join him as soon as possible. After all, I didn't want to miss any more of my time in Australia than could be helped! I watched as he walked away from me, still eye-catching in his well-cut charcoal suit, his blonde hair showing only a few streaks of silver and a striding walk I would know anywhere. He would be fifty-eight this year, but he didn't look it. I knew I would miss him when I returned home without him and I determined to follow him in a matter of days.

I was also keen to be back in the country of my birth, to feel the sun on my face and forget the cold of England for a while. I was looking forward to seeing my best friend, Sandra, whom I hadn't seen since our last trip to Australia, two-and-a-half years ago. Sandra is married to David, whom she met on a cruise that she and I went on together in 1995, sixteen years ago. The same cruise where I met Mike! Would their girls, Avril, now eleven-years-old and Bethany, nine-years-old, still remember us? I couldn't wait to find out.

The real estate agent found a tenant for our house within a couple of days. They were an older couple who had recently arrived from South Africa to join their two grown-up children in London. Forced to flee their farm in order to save their lives, they wanted to rent a house whilst they decided where they would like to buy. It brought home to me the horrors still being experienced in that part of the world. People who had been born there, raised their children, worked hard to make their farm profitable and provided employment for locals, were no longer welcome.

I had the opportunity to meet our tenants when they came to view the house and I was satisfied that they would look after our home in our absence. Charles Richardson was a tall man, athletic-looking, with a shock of light-brown hair which fell across his forehead, accentuating his light blue eyes. His handshake was firm, without being too strong and the twinkle in his eyes indicated that he was a man with a good sense of humour. Jill Richardson was a large woman with a no-nonsense attitude, who raved about our kitchen and said she couldn't wait to start baking in it. I almost felt sorry that I wouldn't be there to sample her cooking!

I booked my flight for the following Sunday and set to work, packing our clothes in boxes and stacking them in the smallest bedroom, along with our personal items. Mike had already moved our files from the study and locked them in a filing cabinet in the same bedroom. I arranged for the gardener we had employed whilst we were in France to take care of the garden for the next twelve months. It was easier to include gardening in the rent than to worry about whether the garden was surviving. I also wanted to make sure that our farming tenants hadn't pulled up my prized bushes to plant vegetables!

James, Mike's eldest son, arrived promptly Sunday morning to drive me to the airport for my early flight. That was the main reason I had booked a Sunday flight; I thought there was a chance that either James or Simon would be able to drive me to the airport and the traffic would be lighter. Like Mike, I had taken full advantage of the baggage allowance as we would not be shipping anything to Australia for this relatively short contract. I planned to buy some lighter clothes in Australia and they would dry very quickly in the heat. James was his usual cheerful self, so like his father and we chatted easily on the way to the airport. Andrea, his partner, was seeing her parents this morning, he explained, otherwise she would have come with him to see me off. I asked James if he was still interested in working in Sydney. As an architect he would have no trouble finding work and, before we went to France for two years, he had shown some interest in moving there.

"I would like to," he responded. "As you know, you piqued my interest in Australia, with all the stories you used to tell us when we were young. Realistically, though, I don't think it's going to happen. I don't see Andrea being happy in Australia, so far from her family and, to be honest, we are both pretty settled in London now."

"I can understand that. Do you think there's any chance you might come to Sydney for a holiday whilst we are there? Free accommodation, you know!"

"I don't know, Anna. I'd like to, but it's a long way to travel unless we can both get at least two weeks off together."

"Well, see what you can do. It would be lovely to spend some time with you both. I can't see Simon and

Kelly making it with young Thomas," I added ruefully.

"You never know – they may surprise you!"

"That would be lovely. Do talk to them and see if you can make it happen."

As I settled into my seat for the long flight home, I thought about how far we would be from Mike's family for the next few months. I recalled the dinner we enjoyed with Mike's parents, Joe and Miranda, the night before Mike left for Australia. As usual, Miranda had cooked a lovely meal, but I think it had dawned on Mike that evening that his parents were starting to show their age. Both in their early eighties they were slowing down and his mother didn't move around the kitchen with her usual ease. He gave her a long hug when he said goodbye and I wondered if he was regretting taking a contract so far from England. Still, the time would pass fairly quickly and by then I imagined Mike's itchy feet would have quietened and he would be content to accept work in London until he retired.

Chapter Three
Back in Sydney!

Mike was waiting for me in the Arrivals Hall at Sydney airport when my plane touched down on Monday evening. I had deliberately picked a flight that would arrive late in the evening so that he could meet me. He grinned broadly and wrapped me in his arms, kissing me enthusiastically.

"How was the flight?" he asked, as he took my suitcase.

"Same as usual – long and tedious. But I'm here now. At least there were no delays – not like your flight."

Poor Mike had experienced a long lay-over in Dubai when the plane he was due to take from there to Australia suffered radar problems and was delayed by nearly four hours.

"I think you'll like the apartment," Mike informed me as we loaded my luggage into his leased car. He had already told me on the phone that he thought I'd be happy with it. Situated in Gladesville, it was only a short bus ride from the city itself and had recently been renovated, so it had a very modern kitchen and bathroom. Such apartments are not easy to come by, but this one had been recommended to him by the personal assistant to his new boss and had made finding accommodation very simple.

We drew up outside a small, new-build apartment block, which I knew had only three apartments. Ours was on the top floor. Although it didn't have a lift, we were both fit enough to manage the stairs.

Inside, Mike left me to look around whilst he took my luggage into the master bedroom. The lounge had a large picture window which looked out on to trees and the gardens. The main bedroom was a very good-sized room, even with my luggage in it. There were only two bedrooms and, although another bathroom would have been nice, the second bedroom was also quite large. The kitchen and bathroom were both brand new and the whole apartment was spacious, light and airy.

"What I didn't tell you, Anna, is that we have our own terrace on top of the apartment!" Mike led me excitedly to the stairs leading to our own private space. A sensor light came on as we stepped out on to the terrace, revealing beautiful outdoor furniture and large pot plants scattered around the terrace. The lights of the city sparkled all around us – it was quite magical.

"There is a wonderful view from here in the day time,

13

looking toward Breakfast Point," he informed me.

"Perfect. I can see us spending a lot of time up here," I enthused. "Wait till Sandra and David see this!"

"So, you think you can be happy here for the next twelve months, Mrs Davies?"

"I'm sure of it," I replied, moving into his open arms.

"Well, let's get you to bed. You must be ready for a good, long sleep."

"I am, but first, a shower," I added.

"I'll probably have left for work by the time you wake up. It's only a ten-minute ride on the bus into the city, so enjoy your first day back home in Australia. Would you like to go out for dinner in the city tomorrow night?"

"That would be lovely. I might join you in the morning, though. It would be nice to have breakfast together."

"Are you hungry now? There's food in the fridge."

"No thanks, I had plenty to eat on the plane. A glass of water and I'll be heading for the shower."

Unfortunately, I didn't wake when Mike rose in the morning and I didn't hear him shower or have his breakfast. It was nearly nine o'clock before I woke and I stretched and kicked off the sheet. It was still warm in

Sydney in April – hot, as our English friends would declare. I sat at the breakfast bar in the kitchen, nursing a coffee and looking out at the trees outside the window. The sun was shining in a very blue sky and magpies were flying in and out amongst the trees. It was so good to be back in Australia!

I picked up my phone and dialled Sandra.

"I'm here!" I exclaimed, as she answered.

"Welcome home, Anna! It's so good to know you are back in Sydney."

"When can I see you?" I asked.

"I kept today free. Why don't I come over to your apartment?"

"That would be awesome!"

"How about this afternoon? That will give you time to unpack some of your things and make yourself at home."

"Perfect. About two? Will you drive?"

"Yes. Public transport is still almost non-existent from Glenhaven and there's plenty of parking in the streets at Gladesville. Two will do nicely. I've arranged for a friend to pick the girls up from school today; we take it in turns anyway. Jenny will look after them until I get home."

"I can't wait to see you! Why don't we make it one o'clock?"

"Suits me. I'll have lunch before I come. I know you won't be organised yet."

"Great. I'll see you then. I'll see if I can rustle up some cake!"

A few minutes before one o'clock there was a rap on the door. I flung it open it to see Sandra, almost hidden behind a large bouquet of pink lilies.

"Sandra, how lovely! Come in."

We fell into each other's arms and hugged, so happy to see each other again.

"Let me look at you!" I said, as we broke apart. I knew from the photos Sandra had sent me of herself and her family that her long red hair had been cut in a shorter style and I thought how much it suited her.

"You haven't changed!" she exclaimed.

"Nor have you - and I love the hair! Thank you so much for the lovely flowers. I'll put the kettle on and find a vase."

"Nice apartment," Sandra commented, taking in the view from the lounge window.

"Yes, we are so lucky. Close to the city and we look

out on to greenery."

Fortunately, the flat possessed two vases, one small and the other large enough to accommodate the lilies, which I quickly arranged and placed on the coffee table in the lounge room.

"I've got a yummy coffee cake too. I caught the bus up to the Gladesville shops and found a great bakery."

We took our cake and coffee into the lounge.

"I wanted to have you to myself," Sandra confessed. "It's been so long. You must come over for lunch on Sunday and see David and the girls, but it's nice to have the chance to catch up by ourselves first."

"I agree; and we'd love to come over for lunch on Sunday!"

The afternoon flew as we chatted non-stop. Although we had spoken on the phone regularly whilst Mike and I were in France, it wasn't the same as talking face-to-face. We studied each other, noting the lines and signs of the years slowly appearing on our faces. Fortunately, time had been kind to both of us and I thought we still looked pretty good for women in their fifties! Sandra liked our apartment, particularly the terrace, where we went with a glass of wine, after we had finished our coffee.

"It's wonderful!" Sandra declared. "What a great space."

"I know. I can't believe it. It's lovely to be warm too!"

"I bet you notice it after England. Have you adjusted to the cold there, Anna?"

"I think you get used to it. I don't like it, but I think I appreciate the warm summer days more because of it."

"I expect you would. Mind you, I always like looking at photos of those gorgeous winter coats in the magazines."

"Yes, I have two winter coats - a black one with a fake fur collar and a cream one. I'd like to get a red one too!"

"It must be wonderful when it snows. You see photos of those little birds with red breasts on English post boxes on Christmas cards."

"The robins. Yes, they are cute and the snow is lovely to look at. It's not so good when it starts to melt though and you are walking in slush!"

"Are you happy, Sandra?" I asked, shortly before she left.

"Yes, I am, Anna. Very. David is a great husband and I adore being a mum. How about you?"

"Yes, I'm happy too. Marrying Mike was the best thing I ever did!"

That evening, Mike and I caught the bus to the city and ate at a restaurant at Darling Harbour. We had a table by the window and looked out on the lights of the city.

"Sydney is so lucky to have so much water around it."

"Yes and it's blue too, not like the brown Thames River. Anyway, tell me about your new job. Are you enjoying it?"

"It's challenging, but so much easier not having to think and speak in French!"

Mike told me about the people he was working with, making me laugh at some of his descriptions, as well as an outline of the work he was undertaking in Sydney. I was pleased he was enjoying it; I wouldn't feel so guilty about my life of leisure.

On Sunday we drove to Glenhaven, noticing the changes in the roads and some of the once-familiar buildings. Glenhaven is semi-rural, very pretty and most of the houses are on large plots of ground. It was a lovely day for a drive. Mike was still getting used to seeing the sun shining brightly nearly every day and revelled in the warm weather. We pulled into Sandra's driveway, admiring the rambling two-storey house, the huge Moreton Bay Fig tree off to one side of their one-acre block and the white roses which grew on either side of the front door. We had barely stopped the car when two young girls burst out of the front door and ran towards us. Both had their mother's red hair, worn long and flying out behind them. I quickly stepped out of the car and opened my arms. Avril reached me first but Bethany was close behind. They hugged me fiercely, before going around the other side of the car to Mike and greeting him in the same way.

"I thought you would have forgotten us by now!" Mike said. "You were so young last time we saw you."

"No, mummy talks about you all the time and shows us your photos." Avril replied.

I couldn't believe how much they had grown. Avril's green eyes were sparkling as she danced around us. I noted that Bethany's eyes were hazel, a mix perhaps of Sandra's green eyes and David's brown?

By now Sandra and David had joined us and I gave Sandra a hug before David wrapped me in his arms.

"It's been too long, you two!" he exclaimed.

"It's so good to see you both again," I told them.

"This calls for a celebration. Come inside and have some champagne." David declared.

Glass in hand, a few minutes later we handed out our souvenirs from London. A doll in a policewoman's outfit for Avril and a beefeater doll, complete with bearskin hat, for Bethany, as well as a London bus and a taxi each. Sandra seemed pleased with her bone china coffee mug from Harrods and we gave David a Harrods water bottle. He enjoyed cycling so we thought it might be useful.

I didn't think David had changed much. His brown eyes were still full of mischief and he was obviously besotted with his daughters.

The afternoon passed quickly, with so much to catch up on and taking time to get to know the girls again. The weather was still warm enough to eat outside and Sandra had prepared a feast for us. Avril was keen to show us her bedroom, decorated in a very pale pink and her collection of china horses. Not to be outdone, Bethany took us to see her pale yellow bedroom and her collection of shells, which she had found at the beach. We stayed until after the girls had showered and come down to say goodnight and the four of us had enjoyed coffee and cake. Reluctantly, we said goodbye to Sandra and David, promising to catch up again soon. It had been a perfect day.

Chapter Four
A Trip is Planned

Life in Australia continued very pleasantly. Mike was enjoying the laid-back attitude of Australians at work after the added stress of having to speak French at work in France. For my part, I was determined that my hard-earned knowledge of the French language was not going to be wasted, so I enrolled in a University of the Third Age French Conversation class. We had made some good friends during our time in France and it was more than likely we would visit them once we returned to live in London. I didn't want to forget my tentative grasp of day-to-day French. I had never managed to become fluent in the two years we spent in the country, but I could manage a reasonable level of conversation and I found I looked forward to these weekly lessons. I also made some new friends at the class, many of whom had visited, or lived, in France at some stage. Not having any family of my own it was nice to make some new friends. I did catch up with a couple of old friends and work colleagues, but it is not easy to pick up the thread when you have been away from Australia for fourteen years.

I went to inspect the house I still owned in the

western suburbs of Sydney, which had been leased by the same family ever since I left Australia. Jane and Mark looked after it as if it was their own. Their son, Dan, who was only a toddler when I last saw him, was a teenager now and had a sister, Therese. Jane welcomed me in and showed me around. Despite having readily agreed to any repairs or maintenance that the real estate agent had suggested over the years, I could see it was in need of more substantial work. It was ready for a new kitchen and bathroom, it badly needed re-painting and one of the fences in the back garden needed to be replaced. I left knowing I had to make a decision as to whether I was going to continue renting the property out, or whether it was time to put it on the market and sell. I knew in my heart that it was very unlikely that I would ever live in Australia again and even if we did, we would be looking for a more substantial house.

I spoke to Mike about it that evening when he came home. He was very much in favour of selling.

"You're never going to live in that house again, Anna and I don't see why you would want the hassle. I think it's time you moved on and let it go. You'll have the money in the bank and won't have the worry."

Deep down I knew he was right, but even so.... it was

a big decision for me to make. The next day I discussed it with Sandra.

"It makes sense, Anna. Mike's right, it's not worth the hassle anymore. Sell!"

And so that afternoon I made the phone call to my tenant, Mark and told him that I had decided to put the house on the market. He didn't seem very surprised. I told him I would speak to the real estate agent the following day but that his lease, which still had a couple of months to run, would of course be honoured. He told me they had been very happy living there but he could understand me wanting to sell it. They had enjoyed a good run and he was sure they would find something else without too much trouble – particularly with the good reference I was going to give them!

About a month after our arrival David and Sandra brought the girls over for Sunday lunch. We had visited them a couple of times, as well as meeting up for lunch in the city, but it was time for me to return their hospitality. I had hired some DVDs from the library for Avril and Bethany to watch, as there was not much for them to do at our apartment. With them safely installed in front of the TV after lunch, we adults took a glass of wine up to the terrace.

"I want to do an outback drive," David told us, stretching out in the sun. "You know, go out west and fossick for some gold or gemstones. I've seen quite a lot of Australia over the years, but I've never been to the real outback. Sandra doesn't want to come and of course, it wouldn't be ideal for the girls. I'm looking for a buddy to come with me." He looked pointedly at Mike.

Mike looked taken aback. I don't think he saw himself as an outback-kind-of-guy. He was more of a city person, complete with suit and, in London, a tie.

"It's no good looking at me, David! Apart from the fact that it's not my idea of a good holiday, I can't get the time off work."

David looked disappointed.

"What's brought this on?" Mike asked.

"I suppose it started when I saw a program on the television, where this couple of guys drove to Central Queensland and went fossicking, travelled across the dessert, camped under the stars, that sort of thing. I realised I was seeing a very different side of Australia. It made me realise that in all these years I have never done anything like that."

"How long are you thinking of going for?" Mike

asked.

David looked at Sandra, rather sheepishly I thought.

"About three weeks, I suppose. It wouldn't be fair to leave Sandra alone with the girls for any longer."

Sandra didn't disagree. If he was looking for a longer dispensation, he was disappointed.

"Never mind, Mike. I thought it was worth asking. I'm sure I can persuade one of the other guys to come with me."

The conversation turned to a new musical playing at The Lyric Theatre and I didn't think any more of David's plans.

A few days later, I received an offer on my house. It was very close to the asking price and I decided to accept, knowing that the property was in need of renovation. Jane and Mark found a more modern house in the same suburb. They invited us over for coffee two days before they moved. Therese, now thirteen, was excited about their new home and sat next to me on the sofa, telling me all about it.

"My bedroom is very large," she told me in a serious voice, "and so is my wardrobe. I'll need some more clothes! And the garden is huge!" She lent closer and whispered. "Mummy said I might be able to have a dog."

"It sounds perfect," I said when she finally ran out of things to say. "I'm sure you will love living there." Satisfied, she disappeared to pack her games into her new suitcase.

Jane and Mark were equally excited about the move and so, in the end, I didn't feel too bad about selling.

It was around this time that David told us that he had found someone to go outback with him. A keen tennis player, David had asked around at the tennis club and Jayden Watson, an electrician by trade, said he had been thinking of going out west again himself. He had made quite a few trips over the years and was a member of a four-wheel drive club, so he had the knowledge which David lacked. Jayden said that he had found a few gemstones some years ago and was quite keen to return to try to find some more. Usually, he travelled with his wife, Emma, but she was reluctant to leave her mother at the present time, as she had recently gone into a nursing home and was having trouble settling in. David knew there were emeralds and sapphires to be found in places called, not surprisingly, Emerald, Sapphire and Rubyvale and he seemed excited to think there was the possibility of combining a vacation with a profit!

Winter is the time to go north or west in Australia, when the temperatures are lower, so plans were immediately put into effect to organise themselves for the trip. They would take Jayden's four-wheel drive as it was already kitted out with everything they would need; a stove for cooking, a small fridge, portable outside shower, a bed for Jayden (David would have to make do with a swag) and room to carry water, a winch and other tools. We were invited for a BBQ to meet Jayden and his wife, Emma.

Jayden, I thought, was a typical country-type Australian. Of medium height and stocky build, he wore an Akubra hat, open-neck shirt, brown shirt, jeans and boots. He had serious, brown eyes beneath very bushy eyebrows. I guessed he would be in his late forties, maybe early fifties, his skin leathered by the sun. His wife's skin was similarly browned by years of exposure to the elements. She too was stockily-built, in her forties, I thought and wore a pair of dark trousers with a green short-sleeved shirt, boots and a thick belt around her ample middle. Her light brown hair was worn very short, showing a few streaks of grey and her hooded eyes darted here and there. I could imagine the pair of them coping with most things that life threw at them. As we sat under the verandah with a gas heater, whilst David barbecued the meat, Emma said she was pleased that Jayden had found someone to go outback with him. Her mother wasn't very well and she hadn't felt able to leave her for over twelve months. Whilst we ate, David and Jayden talked animatedly about their upcoming trip. Avril and Bethany both said they wanted to go with their daddy, but he placated them by saying he would take them when they were older. Sandra rolled her eyes at me. I knew that this was something she was not going to encourage!

Sandra kept me informed of progress over the next couple of weeks as the boys poured over maps and added things to their growing list of provisions. Sandra had been busy pressure- cooking chicken in jars to supplement their food supplies. The chicken would keep for quite a long while. I was looking forward to spending more time with Sandra, Avril and Bethany, to keep them company whilst David was away. Not that I was bored. Apart from dealing with the sale of my house, I was still receiving manuscripts from Don Parker, my boss at Grant & Sons in London, where I had worked as a Senior

Editor before we moved to France. During our time over there, Don had asked me to review the occasional manuscript and I had enjoyed reading and assessing works by both new and established authors. There was no editing involved – I only had to assess their potential to make money! The arrangement suited me very well and was continuing whilst I was in Australia, so I had plenty of books to read and I found the work stimulating. I had received a manuscript this week by Lizzie Tranton, whose first book, 'Something in the Air', was a best-seller. I was involved with her when I was in France, helping her to leave an unsuitable boyfriend and return to London to finish writing the book, so I couldn't wait to see if her latest book was equally as good.

It wasn't long before everything was ready for David and Jayden's departure and Sandra cooked a special lunch for David the day before they were due to leave and invited us to join them. They would be leaving on the twelfth of July. You could see that David was excited about this adventure, promising to bring his three girls back a sapphire or emerald each. Mike quietly reminded him that he was only planning to be away for three weeks! No doubt he would buy them something, if he didn't find the promised gems himself!

I received a phone call from Sandra the following evening to let me know they had left early that morning and that she was missing David already. It was the first time they had been apart since they were married. I promised to call in the next day for coffee.

Chapter Five
Overdue

Sandra and I spent a lot of time together over the next three weeks. Mike and I invited her and the girls over for lunch on Sundays and I would see her every second or third day whilst Avril and Bethany were at school. Sometimes we would go out for a coffee but we also managed to revisit many of Sydney's sights. Together we laughed our way around the Museum of Contemporary Art (neither of us having any appreciation for modern art) and gawked at the splendid opulence during a tour of the old State Theatre. We took a ride on the ferry to Manly, walking through the Corso from the protected waters where the ferry comes in to the surf on the other side. We bought fish and chips and coffee and sat on the front watching the waves pounding on to the sand. We admired the surfers as they tackled the monster waves and watched people walking back and forth along the beach. We also wandered around the famous Rocks area, which contains some of Sydney's original houses, as well as many little boutique shops. It was lovely to have this time with Sandra after our long separation. It took us back to the carefree days of our youth, when we would spend hours together, doing nothing in particular.

David had rung to say they were now in Queensland and travelling well, apart from a leaking radiator hose, which they had fixed in Toowoomba. He rang again from Emerald, as soon as they arrived. He said that Jayden was a good travelling companion and that he was excited at the prospect of fossicking for emeralds.

A few days later he had rung from Rubyvale, where they were fossicking for rubies. Sandra asked if they had found anything worthwhile and he had replied not much, only a few very small gems, but that he was enjoying the experience. The next call was from Longreach, on the thirtieth of July, where they had visited the Stockman's Hall of Fame and the Qantas Museum, both of which he had found very impressive. He told her they were going on to Winton, to see the dinosaur footprints. He tried to explain the landscape to her.

"You can drive for kilometres and see only bush and dirt and, in some places, the dirt is so red it hurts your eyes when the sun reflects off it. It gets into everything and it stains your clothes. There are mobs of kangaroos bounding around too. They'll jump across the road in front of you, so you have to keep a good look-out for them."

Sandra didn't think this sounded like much of a holiday, but it was David's choice. He did say that he didn't know when he would be able to contact her again, as they would be in the bush with no reception for much of the time. Even so, she was disappointed when she didn't hear from him again over the next few days.

"I had hoped he would be missing me!" she complained when she came over for lunch.

"I'm sure he is, Sandra. I expect it's very difficult, that's all, with so little phone reception. Anyway, he'll be home soon." Mike replied.

"Well, he could have rung to tell me which day he is coming," she grumbled.

I could see that she wasn't convinced, so I decided it was time to serve dessert. I knew my tiramisu would appeal to her sweet tooth and take her mind off David for a while.

I was thrilled to discover that Lizzie Tranton's latest book, "Bluebells in the Spring", was as good as her first book. I had wondered if she would continue with her writing, or if she would become caught up with life and put it aside. So often an author has a best-seller and then disappears, either for several years or never to be heard of again. Remembering my experience with Lizzie in France, I had worried that she would fall by the wayside, but it seems Lizzie is serious about making writing her career and I was delighted for her. I reported back to Don and asked him to pass on my congratulations to her. I was sure she had written another best-seller.

Sandra became more and more tense as the third week of David's trip progressed. Not knowing exactly when he would be returning home, she helped the girls to make "Welcome home, Daddy," banners, which they put up on the front verandah at the end of the three weeks. Two days later there was still no sign of David and not even a phone call. We had all tried to ring him, but the message was always the same "this phone is switched off or out of range." By now, Sandra was becoming exasperated.

"He could at least have called me," she ranted over the phone. "He's never this thoughtless. He knows we are all waiting to see him. I don't understand why we haven't heard anything from him to say when he'll be home. They must be back within phone range by now."

"Have you spoken to Emma?"

Yes, every day! I rang her about three days before they were due to come home and I've been ringing her ever since. She hasn't heard from Jayden either."

"Did she sound worried?"

"No, not at all. She said it was quite normal for things to happen and you couldn't have a timetable for these sorts of trips. They'd turn up safe and sound in due course."

"But doesn't David have to go back to work?"

"Not until next week. He knew the trip could take longer than they expected, so he allowed himself a few more days."

When Sandra still hadn't heard from David by Monday, I suggested that maybe she should make a report at the police station.

"What, a missing person's report! He's a grown man. Anyway, he's not missing, he's just not....not.....here!" she spluttered.

"But it's totally out of character for David, isn't it?"

"Well, yes. There again, he's never been on an outback trip before. It's not all about him either, it's Jayden's trip as well. Maybe they got side-tracked somewhere. They could have broken down," she added lamely.

I persuaded her to talk to Emma and suggested they report the boys as missing. Emma wasn't concerned and thought that Sandra was panicking, but she agreed, somewhat reluctantly, to accompany her. They went to Sandra's local police station that afternoon and lodged a report. The middle-aged policeman behind the desk, who took down the details, didn't seem very concerned.

"People get lost or break down in the bush all the time. Eventually they find their way home. Everyone helps everyone else in the outback. If they've broken down, as long as they stay with their vehicle, someone will come along sooner or later and give them a hand," he informed them.

"That's what I've been telling her," Emma said.

"But you will try to make some enquiries?" Sandra asked.

"Yes, madam, I will. I'll make sure the authorities in Central Queensland are alerted to keep a look-out for them."

Thanking him, they made their way outside to Sandra's car. At Glenhaven, Sandra made some coffee and they talked about the likelihood of something having happened to their husbands.

"I can't help thinking about that serial killer, Ivan Milat," Sandra said.

"Well, he's in jail now, so we don't have to worry about him," Emma replied.

"Yes, but these things do happen. What if they have been hurt?"

"They wouldn't both be hurt, Sandra. One of them would be able to go for help. Anyway, I'm sure it's nothing like that. They've probably broken down somewhere. Like the policeman said, they'd be waiting for someone to come along and give them a lift."

"I hope they have plenty of water."

"My Jayden's very particular about that. He always carries plenty of water."

Emma drained her cup and stood up to leave.

"We'll keep in touch. Try not to worry too much, Sandra. Jayden's a very good bushman. Your David couldn't be in more capable hands."

Chapter Six
The Search Begins

Another night passed without a word from Jayden or David and Sandra was becoming frantic. When I arrived at her house shortly after lunch she burst into tears. I gave her a hug and she cried all over me. I led her to the sofa and waited whilst she wiped her eyes and blew her nose.

"David would never let me worry like this, he knows I'd be frantic by now."

"I'm sure you'll hear from him as soon as he can contact you."

"He was due back at work yesterday. He's not an irresponsible person; this is so out of character. Something must have happened to them, Anna."

"I know, Sandra. Something's wrong, but I'm sure it's not as serious as you are thinking. You spoke to the office I suppose, to see if they had heard from him?"

"They rang here first thing in the morning, before I had a chance to ring them, wanting to know why he hadn't returned to work. Apparently, there's a big job on and they need him. I told them I hadn't heard from him, but I'd be in touch as soon as I knew something. They

39

seemed quite concerned too. Oh, Anna, it is so awful! I think even Emma is starting to worry now."

I left her sitting on the sofa and went out to the kitchen to find a bottle of wine. There was an open bottle of sauvignon blanc in the fridge and I poured us both a glass.

"Here, drink this. It will help to settle you."

"I can't concentrate on anything, Anna," she said as she took a large mouthful, quickly followed by another. "I have an important report to finish for work by tomorrow and I can't seem to concentrate on it." She put down the glass of wine. "I'd better not have any more of that until I've done it."

"Why don't I pick the girls up from school and stay whilst you finish your report. I'll cook dinner and you can work through."

She flashed me a grateful smile. "Thanks, Anna. That might help. I'll go into the study now and see if I can knuckle down and keep my mind on writing this report."

I looked in the fridge to see what I could cook for dinner. I decided on Spaghetti Bolognese. All children like spaghetti, don't they? Sandra had a jar of sauce, a full packet of spaghetti and plenty of vegetables. I chopped the vegetables and put the spaghetti into a dish with some salt, ready to microwave. For the next hour I answered some emails on my phone and flicked through a couple of magazines that were on the coffee table.

"I'm going to pick up the girls now," I said, popping my head around the study door. "It looks as if you're immersed in that report. I'll buy some mince for the Spaghetti Bolognese at the same time. Is there anything else you want?"

"Just some milk, please," she replied, lifting her eyes from the screen for a few seconds and flashing me a smile. "Yes, the report's going well. I should be done by dinner-time."

Bethany and Avril were delighted to have their Aunt Anna pick them up from school.

"Where's Mum?" Bethany wanted to know as soon as she was buckled into the car seat.

"She's working on a report for work. We're going to stop at the shops for some mince and some milk. I'm going to cook dinner tonight - Spaghetti Bolognese – is that okay?"

"Yes!" they both answered. "That's my favourite," Avril informed me.

We stopped at the local store and they chose some lollies to keep them going until dinner time. It was wonderful to be an aunt and to be in Australia to spoil them.

The girls ran in to the study to receive a kiss from their mum.

"Okay, why don't we go and play with your dolls in the family room?" I suggested.

"Yes, that's an excellent idea!" Bethany exclaimed. "My Susan needs to change into her best dress, ready for Daddy coming home."

I had rung Mike and suggested that he warm up some left-over casserole that was in the fridge, for his evening meal.

With her report finished, Sandra came into the kitchen in time for us to enjoy a glass of wine before we ate. It was a happy, noisy meal as the girls talked over each other to tell their mum what they had been doing at school. As David sometimes travelled for work, both within Australia and in Asia, Avril and Bethany were used to his occasional absences so, fortunately, they were not unduly upset that he wasn't at home. We were enjoying some ice-cream when the phone rang. When Sandra returned, I could see that she had tears in her eyes.

"That was someone from the police station to say that the Queensland police are taking our report seriously and they have put out a general alert for our men."

"That's great! Someone is taking their absence seriously then."

"They mentioned that another young couple from Melbourne seem to have gone missing in that area too."

"See, people go missing all the time in the outback!" I quickly pointed out.

Sandra managed a small smile.

"Time for a quick cartoon before bed," I announced. The girls quickly finished their ice-cream and I went into the lounge with them to help them select a video.

"I wonder if David and Jayden's disappearance is linked with the other couple?" I mused to myself, as I cleared the dishes.

"Don't say that! You'll have me imagining a serial killer running around out there!"

"Only kidding," I said quickly, realising my mistake. I busied myself loading the dishwasher.

"Will you be okay now, Sandra?" I asked, preparing to leave.

"The evenings are the worst. You know, after the girls have gone to bed. I know I'm being pathetic, but it's so lonely and I spend my time wondering where David can be," she said plaintively.

She looked so forlorn, I gave her a quick hug and suggested I stay for the evening.

"We can talk about old times and that might help you forget for a while," I suggested.

The tears came then and I put my arm around her shoulders.

"It'll be okay, Sandra. They will find them soon. Someone will come across them."

When the tears stopped, she said "I should ring Emma. I'm sure she's as devastated as I am."

Her phone was next to her handbag on the bench. I stood up and passed it to her.

"Hi, Emma. How are you? I know, they rang me. It's good that they are taking this seriously. Yes, I know it's a huge area to search. I do have faith in Jayden, Emma, it's because it's been so long and it's so unlike David. He knows how much I worry and he wouldn't leave it this long to speak to his girls if he could get through. Anyway, the police asked me for David's credit card details and his mobile phone number. They're going to see when they were last used. Did they ask you the same thing? I guessed they would. Yes, of course I'll keep in touch. I'm glad you are not worrying too much."

Sandra was quiet for a few moments. "I think she's more worried than she lets on. She says she isn't overly concerned; she knows how easy it is for something to go wrong. She's convinced that whatever it is, Jayden can handle it. I can only hope that Jayden hasn't been taken ill."

By now the police were starting to take Sandra's daily calls seriously. They had spoken to David's office and to some of their friends, including me and Emma and confirmed that this was totally out of character for both David and Jayden. Although Australia is a huge country with some very isolated and dangerous outback country, many people ventured into the outback now, due to improved vehicles with increased water and fuel carrying capacity. Unless they were deep in the bush, it seemed unlikely that no-one had come across them, if they had broken down. The last activity on David's credit card was when he paid for entry into the Winton Age of Dinosaurs Museum on July 30 and the last entry on Jayden's was for petrol at a place called Dingo on August 1. Neither of their mobile phones had been used after July 30. That meant the police were concentrating their search around Longreach and Winton. Jayden had taken a couple of phone calls in the week prior, but they were work-related. The police had spoken to both of the callers, but both said that Jayden had only said he was on holiday and made no mention of where they were going.

I spent the next evening with Sandra and the girls. We played games with Avril and Bethany and tried not to let them sense that anything was wrong. As far as they were concerned, Daddy was still away on holiday. However, in the middle of a game of snakes and ladders, Avril broke off from shaking the dice and looked up at her mother.

"When is Daddy going to ring us, Mummy?"

Sandra glanced over at me. "I don't know, sweetheart. I don't think they have any mobile phone connection where he is. I'll make sure he speaks to you when he does ring."

Satisfied for the time being, Avril threw the dice and the game continued.

Around ten o'clock I said goodnight to Sandra and headed for home. On the drive, I wondered what could have had happened to David and Jayden. I had an uneasy feeling about their disappearance in the pit of my stomach, which was becoming stronger as the days passed.

Chapter Seven
A Plan is Hatched

"Where do you start looking for two missing guys in a country the size of Australia?" I asked Mike, as soon as I arrived home.

"Good question. Actually, it isn't the whole of Australia, is it? Presumably, they are still somewhere in Queensland."

"That's still a big area. I looked it up - it's five times the size of Great Britain!"

"It probably is. Still.....we do have a rough idea of where they were going."

"The police said they would keep making inquiries to see if anyone had seen them. They could have fallen down a disused mine shaft, for all we know."

"That's not impossible, but surely they wouldn't both have fallen down one?"

"You're always so logical! Well, what if they found a huge emerald or sapphire and someone killed them for it?"

"Anna! Now you are letting your imagination run away with you. Firstly, the chances of finding a huge emerald or sapphire are fairly small. Secondly,

Queensland isn't the Wild West. David is a fairly conservative type, he isn't going to go around telling everyone about a big find and shouting the bar and I think Jayden is pretty switched on too, so he wouldn't either."

"I hope you're right," I replied, feeling a bit miffed. "Emma is still not too concerned apparently, but Sandra is very upset."

"I expect she is. How are the girls?"

"They still think Daddy is away on holiday, so they aren't worried at all, although Avril did ask when he was going to ring them."

"What did Sandra say?"

"She said he was probably out of range and that seemed to satisfy them for the time being."

I didn't sleep well that night. I tossed and turned and, when I finally fell asleep, I dreamt that David was down the bottom of a mine shaft, hurt and bleeding, screaming for help and trying to claw his way out.

Over breakfast I voiced the thought that had occupied my mind for most of those unslept hours.

"I'm thinking that maybe I should go and try to find David – for Sandra's sake."

"What? Are you mad? Have you ever even been in the outback? No, I thought not," Mike said as I shook my head in the negative. "How is a city girl like you going to manage out there?"

"I thought Emma might come with me. She knows nearly as much as Jayden does about the outback."

"Have you forgotten your promise to me?" he asked, almost belligerently. "You promised me that you would never again become involved in any mysteries. A promise you made only a few months ago, I might remind you."

His eyes were ablaze with anger and I knew I should proceed cautiously.

"No, of course I haven't forgotten, darling - and I meant it too. But this is different: surely you're not going to hold me to that when my best friend's husband is missing?" I wheedled.

I saw a fleeting sign of weakening. I decided to press home my point.

"This isn't like those other mysteries. You said yourself there is unlikely to be any danger. I want to retrace the steps we know they took and to talk to people – lots of people – and see if we can track their movements. After all, I have time that the police don't."

Mike ran his fingers through his short, blonde hair. He was even more attractive when he frowned.

"I don't know, Anna. I don't like it. You don't even know where to start. Queensland is huge; you said so yourself. Somehow, you always seem to get caught up in these things and you know I can't take time off work to go with you."

"Well, your outback skills are a bit wanting too, coming as you do from London. Overall, I think I'd rather take my chances with Emma."

That last comment extracted a small smile.

"Okay, point taken. Well, see if Emma is prepared to go with you. If she is, I guess I'll have to release you from your promise. As you say, Sandra is your best friend. But only this one time and only if Emma is prepared to go with you!"

"Definitely." I stood up and went to him, surprising him with a passionate kiss.

"I'll ring Emma as soon as I've tidied the kitchen."

Emma said she had been having similar thoughts herself. It was approaching a week past the boys' anticipated return and she hadn't heard anything from Jayden.

"Obviously Sandra can't leave the house to go looking for David. She has the girls to take care of and, anyway, she wants to be there for David when he comes home," I explained, somewhat unnecessarily. "I'd be happy to look for him, but I have no experience in the outback; in fact, I haven't even been camping! But I thought, if you wanted to go and look for Jayden, perhaps I could come with you?"

"Well, I must admit I have been thinking about it. It's not like Jayden not to be in touch. I don't like to leave my mother, but the nursing home takes great care of her and, in fact, she wouldn't know whether I've been there five minutes or five weeks before. It's probably more important for me to go and look for Jayden. But I think you would be more of a hindrance to me than a help. Probably best you stay here and I'll go."

That wasn't what I wanted to hear.

"I promise I'll try very hard not to be a nuisance. I know that I have no knowledge of the outback or even camping, to be honest, but I'm sure I'll get the hang of it. Also, I do have quite a record of solving mysteries, going back some years. I think that is where I may be of some use."

"Solving mysteries? What sort of mysteries? Finding

your husband's socks, or something?"

I forced a laugh. "No. Well, yes, but that's not what I meant. I discovered what happened to some missing children in France, discovered the killer of my missing author in London, found out what happened to a woman who went overboard from a cruise and helped to find the missing brother of my boyfriend of the time, in Egypt."

"I see. Well, that's pretty impressive, I guess. Something you can tell me more about on our long drive. You're right, I don't have much experience in solving those sorts of mysteries but, hopefully, we won't need to use your skills in finding these boys. I'm expecting to find that they broke down somewhere. Maybe one of them is injured. By now, someone would have found them and helped them and they are probably staying somewhere pretty isolated and they can't contact us. As soon as they have recovered enough to move on, or their vehicle has been repaired, they'll be in touch. Not much mystery about that!"

She laughed, a deep throaty laugh that made me smile too.

"Okay. It's always safer to travel with someone. Can you be ready in a couple of days? I'll have to borrow a campervan from one of our friends and get some supplies together. It will give the boys time to get home. No point us driving all that way if they're already on their way back!"

So, reluctantly, Emma agreed to take me along with her. She arranged to borrow a campervan from a friend and set to gathering stores and bedding. I agreed to finance the trip, as my part of the arrangement and began to pack some clothes. I knew enough to pack some long-sleeved shirts to protect me from the sun, as by now it would be getting pretty hot in the outback, a wide-brimmed hat, some shorts and long trousers. On Emma's advice, I bought a pair of stout boots, something I wouldn't normally possess! I also put in a couple of jumpers and bought a tracksuit for the cold nights, which I had been warned about. Emma rang back late in the morning the next day.

"The campervan is stocked, Anna. Can you be ready at six in the morning and I'll come and pick you up. Let's go and find these men."

I quickly rang Sandra to tell her that we would be leaving in the morning.

"Oh, do be careful, Anna. Don't let anything happen to you."

"I won't. Like Emma says, they must have broken

down and are staying somewhere out of range. They are probably waiting on parts for the vehicle. I do hope we can find them. It's such a huge area to search."

"I feel a bit better already, knowing you are going out to look for David. Sitting here doing nothing is so hard, especially when I have to put on a brave face for the girls' sake. I don't know how I'm going to manage without you to cheer me up but, at the same time, I'm glad you are going to do something."

"You can always ring Mike, you know that. He'll be happy to give you and the girls any support you need."

"Yes, I know. Give David our love when you find him and a hug and a big kiss. Please try to keep in touch."

I could hear in her voice that she was choking back tears, so I quickly said goodbye and ended the call.

Next, I rang Mike at work and told him that we were setting off early the next day.

"I'll cook you something nice for dinner," I promised. "You know I've been cooking, in-between packing, and I've frozen a few meals, so you have something to eat if you don't feel like cooking."

"Yes, I know and I appreciate it. I do still remember how to cook though."

"I know, but it helps me to feel less guilty about going

off and leaving you!"

After a pleasant evening, I tossed and turned all night, worrying if I would be able to cope with Emma and the different lifestyle. I knew I was more the hotel-and-luxury-bathroom-type than a camper. The thought of red dust and limited water didn't appeal at all. Then I remembered Sandra's distress, how much she loved David and how much his family needed him and I resolved to cope with whatever came my way.

At six o'clock on the dot, Emma pulled into our driveway. The campervan was quite modern, I noted, but it was smaller than I had imagined. Better for manoeuvering, no doubt. Mike carried my two bags to the vehicle, passing them to Emma to store. Wrapping me in his arms he gave me a long, deep kiss.

"Come back to me soon, Anna," he whispered. "I'll miss you. Take care, both of you."

I climbed into the passenger seat and Emma reversed. Before I knew it, we were off on our outback adventure.

Chapter Eight
On the Road

Our first day on the road seemed very long to me. I kept glancing around at the area behind the front seats. It was quite modern, I was pleased to note and I assured myself that it would have everything we needed. It wasn't very big, though. Emma wanted to make it to Queensland as soon as possible. She drove for nearly four hours before pulling into a layby.

"We might have that cup of coffee you've got in the thermos now," she declared. "Then you can drive for a bit."

We hadn't talked much on the way. I had asked Emma about the trips she had done out in the bush and she told me she had been all the way to Cooktown once, which is near the very top of Queensland, to Darwin in the Northern Territory and over to Broome in Western Australia another time, all with Jayden, apart from numerous shorter trips. She told me she could fish, shoot rabbits (goodness, had she brought a gun with her on this trip?) and find bush tucker. She and Jayden had spent some time with the Aboriginals in various parts of the country, learning about their culture and how to find food in the bush, so she assured me that we wouldn't starve if our supplies ran out.

The campervan didn't handle as well as the sedans I had always driven, but the road was good and I soon adjusted to it. After a couple of hours, we pulled over again and ate the sandwiches I had packed and finished the coffee. Fifteen minutes later we were ready to continue. Emma insisted on taking the wheel again.

"I drive a bit faster than you, so we'll get there quicker," was her reasoning.

The coastal scenery was pretty and I enjoyed the drive through the popular areas of Port Macquarie, Ballina and Lennox Heads. The glimpses of the sea were stunning – deep blue water, shimmering in the sun, with white sea horses cantering across the waves. Now popular with retirees as places to retire to, they had grown considerably since I had last seen them in my childhood and early teens. Once we got into northern NSW the scenery changed to lusher, greener foliage. The temperature increased, it was quite humid and the sun burned down on us from a clear blue sky.

Ten hours after we left Sydney, we arrived at Tweed Heads on the border of Queensland and New South Wales and slipped quietly into the State where we hoped to find Jayden and David. We found a camping ground at Coolangatta and Emma expertly manoeuvred the vehicle into its spot.

"It's got an awning that pulls out to give us room for a fold-up table and chairs outside, but we won't bother about that tonight. We might prefer to eat outside in future, that way we can leave the bed made up. They've got a bit of a restaurant here, so we might go and eat there, save our food. Right now, I'll show you around the campervan!"

I was glad to be out of the vehicle and able to stretch and walk around. It was much warmer here than Sydney and I was glad of it. Emma opened the campervan's sliding door and I had my first proper look inside. There was a sink, a microwave and stove. She showed me how the table and benches converted to a bed and where the bedding was stored. I looked in dismay at the double bed. It hadn't occurred to me that we wouldn't have twin beds.

"Don't worry, love," Emma said, noticing the look on my face. "Living so close to each other in the bush, sharing a bed is going to be the least of your worries! You'll soon get used to it."

I very much doubted it, but I remembered Sandra

back at home with Avril and Bethany, anxiously awaiting news of David.

The caravan park was quite busy and I could see a lot of people sitting outside their caravans with a glass of wine or beer.

"It's Happy Hour now," Emma stated. "People get together and tell stories of their travels over a beer or two. It's a good time to learn about the road ahead, places to see and maybe even our missing travellers." She opened the small fridge and produced a couple of cans of beer.

"Here," she said, handing me one. "Now we are ready to go and join them."

I followed Emma outside as she walked up to the people parked next to us.

"How you going?" she inquired.

"Good mate and you? Want to sit here for a while?" he asked, pointing to a couple of empty chairs, which I was guessing he had put out for the purpose.

"That would be nice. I'm Emma and this here is Anna."

"Frank and Irene," the man replied. He had a dark, bushy beard, thick eyebrows and brown eyes. His was thin, with a tanned face, deeply lined by the sun and wore shorts and an old t-shirt. Irene had short, brown hair, a full round face and her ample body was encased in a long, flowery dress.

Emma, Frank and Irene exchanged stories for half-an-hour or so, whilst I listened. They offered us another beer, but Emma declined, saying we were going to make an early start in the morning. She pulled out one of our many copies of the photo of Jayden and David taken the morning they left, standing next to the slide-on camper.

"Don't suppose you've seen these two fellas on your travels?"

Irene took a look at the photo, shaking her head and passing it to Frank.

"Sorry, can't say we have. Why are you looking for them?"

"They've gone missing. Went for a holiday and haven't made it home. Jayden's my husband, Anna is a friend of David's wife. We're on our way to try and find them. They were last heard of in Longreach, but goodness knows where they may have gone from there."

"Won't be easy to find them," Frank commented, "if you don't know where to start."

"No, it won't, but we're going to try," Emma responded.

"The vehicle is pretty distinctive, though," Frank added. "Sometimes people notice the type of camper you are driving, more than the occupants!"

Frank and Irene wished us luck in our search and we walked around the caravan park, showing the photo to others enjoying Happy Hour, without any luck.

Eventually, we made our way across to the restaurant. Whilst I studied the menu, Emma asked the girl behind the counter the same question. She was unable to help but did take the photo to show to the other girl working with her, but she couldn't recollect seeing them either.

"Not surprising, really," Emma said as we sat down at a table by the window. "I doubt they would have stopped here anyway. Jayden probably stayed in NSW the first night and then drove right past here."

My fish and chips were quite good and Emma seemed to enjoy her chicken parmigiana. Then it was time to check out the ablutions block. It was better than I had expected, quite large and clean, with plenty of hot water. When I returned to the campervan, freshly showered, I rang Mike and Sandra.

"We've made it in to Queensland. We're not far from the border, in a caravan park," I told Mike. "How are things with you?"

"Good. I worked late tonight, so I've only been in a few minutes. I'm about to defrost one of your frozen meals."

Sandra was sitting down with a cup of coffee, the girls fast asleep in bed.

"This is the worst time of the day," she told me. "I'm here all alone, wondering where the hell David is."

"Hopefully we'll have some news for you soon."

"I know. I wish I was with you. No, actually, I don't, because then I'd be wondering if David had come home to an empty house."

"And you have the girls to think about. Try not to worry too much, Sandra. I'm sure he'll be home soon."

"I hope so. Good luck, Anna and thank you."

Emma let me climb into bed first (which meant I had to climb over her if I wanted to go to the toilet) and we said goodnight. It felt very strange to be sharing a bed with someone other than Mike. I made sure I kept well over my side of the bed, but I must have slept well because the next thing I knew Emma was telling me it was time to get up. We had a good breakfast of bacon and eggs in the restaurant and were on the road by seven-thirty.

We drove west of Brisbane, out to Toowoomba on the New England Highway. It was cooler here, being higher in altitude, but not as cold as Sydney at this time of year. In Toowoomba we bought take-away coffees and sandwiches and showed the woman behind the counter our photograph. She took a quick look at it and said that she couldn't remember seeing either of them.

"Do you think it's worth showing the photo around in Toowoomba before we leave?" I asked Emma as we ate our sandwiches in a local park.

"I suppose it wouldn't hurt. For all we know, they could have passed through here again on their way home."

We split up. I went to the chemists, supermarkets and petrol stations. Emma headed off to the pubs. An hour or so later we met up again back at the campervan.

"No luck?" I asked.

"Nothing. How about you?"

"The same."

"Okay then, let's head off to Roma."

We took the Warrego Highway and drove straight through to Roma, arriving at midday. The traffic wasn't too heavy and I was delighted to see lots of kangaroos on the way, large mobs in paddocks, grazing and resting. Later on in our trip, we would see dead kangaroos on the side of the road, having been hit by a car or a truck trying to cross the road. We also saw lots of 'grey nomads', the term given to retirees with their caravans and mobile homes, who had come up from the southern States to enjoy the warmer weather in Queensland. After we had booked into a caravan park, Emma and I again went separate ways, armed with our photos. There was a good chance that Jayden and David had stopped at Roma and we were keen to find someone who had seen them. This was my first visit to an outback town, but with a population of around seven thousand people, it was much like any suburban town. I did see a huge bottle tree, nearly ten metres around its girth which, the plaque told me, had been transplanted from a local property back in 1927.

When we met up again, I had drawn blanks, but Emma had spoken to a man behind the bar at one of the pubs, who remembered seeing our boys.

"According to him, they stopped in for a couple of beers, but that was some time back. Must have been on the way out."

"Well, at least someone recognised them!"

We spoke to a few people in the caravan park. I was amazed at how far some of them had travelled and how long they had been on the road. Most of them were grey nomads, but a few were young couples, some with small children. A few were travelling around the whole of Australia in one trip; one couple were on their third trip around Australia. Such a different way of life, I thought. None of them remembered seeing Jayden or David, although many of them had been to Emerald.

We decided to eat at one of the pubs that evening and we both had a very large steak, seeing as how we were in cattle country, with chips and salad. Despite not having done much exercise, I found all this travelling made me hungry. We finished with sticky date pudding for me and pavlova for Emma. None of the staff remembered seeing Jayden or David.

Before we went to bed, I rang Mike.

"How's it going?" he asked. "Did you make it to Roma?"

"Yes, we did. It never occurred to me I'd be sharing a double bed with Emma. I thought we'd have our own beds!"

"I wondered if you had thought about that. At least she won't snore – you're always complaining about my

66

snoring!"

"Want to bet? She's worse than you!"

"Good! You won't complain about me again!"

"We've been pretty tired at night, so I've slept okay, but it is very strange to wake up with someone else after all these years."

"Well, at least I don't have that trouble, waking up alone," he moaned. "I do miss you, Anna."

"Miss you too. Hopefully it won't be long before we are on our way back. A man in one of the pubs remembers seeing Jayden and David some time ago, so I guess that was on their way north. We spoke to a few people in the caravan park but no-one there remembers seeing them."

"It will be hard, but you knew that before you left. I'm sure you'll find out something when you get further along the road."

Sandra was pleased to hear my voice.

"Hi, Anna. How's it going? How far did you get today?"

"We're at Roma, administrative centre of the Maranoa region, in case you don't know! Have you heard anything?"

"No, nothing. I know it's too soon for you to have learned anything. What's Roma like?"

"It's okay. Bigger than I expected. It's cold now, but it was warm enough during the day. I saw the big bottle tree it's famous for; that's pretty impressive. A bartender in one of the pubs remembers seeing David and Jayden a few weeks ago – that must have been on their way north, but, so far, no-one else has recognised them."

"You'd have to be lucky, I guess. I hate not being able to see you. How are things going with Emma?"

"Fine. She talks a lot and she snores, but otherwise we are getting on okay."

We chatted for a few more minutes and then I said goodnight.

I didn't sleep as well that night. I was very conscious of Emma lying next to me and when I did doze off it was to be woken by the sound of her snoring! *Great*, I thought. *This was going to be quite a trip.* I must have drifted off eventually, because it was light when I opened my eyes again and Emma was already up and making coffee.

"That smells good," I told her.

"Well, hop up and put the bed away so I can put it on the table."

I did as I was bid and we sat drinking our coffee companionably.

"It's about four hundred kilometres from here to Emerald, so we'll be there about lunchtime, all going well," Emma informed me.

"Then the serious business starts."

"Then the serious business starts," she confirmed.

When we rolled into Emerald later that afternoon, I was surprised to find that it was quite a large town, with all the usual amenities. I had expected it to be a small village. The landscape had become drier and browner as we headed north and, in my mind's eye, I had imagined a one-horse town with nothing more than a pub and a general store, although Emma had assured me it was quite civilised. We found a caravan park in the town, as well as a café where we enjoyed a late lunch. We showed the photo of the boys to the waitress, but she laughed and said that so many people came and went in Emerald they would need to have done something to make themselves stand out, for anyone to remember them. I hoped that some of the other town's inhabitants were more observant. She did have a good suggestion to make though, that we should check whether they had taken out a fossicking licence. We knew they had been fossicking so, after having something to eat, we headed off to the tourist office where they also sold fossicking licences. Emma seemed pretty sure that Jayden wouldn't have bought one on line, but would have made for the tourist office.

An elderly volunteer listened to our request and we showed him a photo of Jayden and David. He thought he remembered seeing them, but he couldn't be sure. He searched through his record of issued licences and found a one-month licence, the shortest time possible, in Jayden's name. He pushed his glasses back on his nose as he spread a map of the area on the table in front of us and showed us the area covered by the licence. I had expected the licence to relate to a designated area – a patch of land that was temporarily leased only to the licence holder. Instead, it covered quite a large area. These were general licences to fossick in any of the designated areas, not for a particular plot of ground. It didn't help us very much in our search, apart telling us they had a licence to fossick for a whole month. Perhaps they had stopped here again on their way home for one more try at finding that big emerald?

"We need to talk to as many people here as we can," I said to Emma as we sat in the campervan waiting for Happy Hour to commence. We need to find someone who talked to the boys and might know what their plans were."

"We know that they went to Sapphire and Rubyvale before they went to Longreach. It's going to be a big job," Emma replied with a sigh. "Most people who would have been here at that time would have moved on by now. We'll ask around the caravan park, but I think we need to try to find people who live here and hope that the boys talked to one of them."

We wandered around the caravan park later, with a beer in our hands, talking to people and showing them the photo. No-one we spoke to had seen Jayden or David.

"I've had an idea," I said much later as we prepared for bed. "Why don't we take this to the local radio station? They can put out a call for anyone who has seen or spoken to them. Then we can pin up some of these photos around town with a number to contact. Maybe we can get people to come to us, rather than us chasing all over the place."

"That's a great idea, Anna. I'm glad I brought you along, after all. Could save us a lot of running around. We'll contact them first thing in the morning."

I walked over to the ablutions block with my soap and towel, hoping I wouldn't have to visit it again during the night. After my shower, I rang Mike.

"How's the search going?" he wanted to know.

I filled him in on our day.

"We know that David and Jayden took out a fossicking licence on the fifteenth of July, which lasted for a month, so they might have come back here for another try. I'm going to the local radio station in the morning, to see if they will run a story about them. I think that could be the best way to reach anyone who has seen them. You know, get them to come to us, rather than us trying to find someone who remembers the boys."

"Brilliant idea, Anna! Good to know you are using your head. I hope you get something from it."

Next, I rang Sandra, who hadn't heard anything from the police. She was thrilled to hear that something was going to be put over the air in Emerald.

"That's wonderful, Anna. Well done. Make sure you

let me know what you find out."

In the meantime, Emma had rung the nursing home where her mother lived and was relieved to learn that her mother had not missed her visits. Relieved, she walked over to the toilet block, before we retired for the night.

"Ever seen a koala in the wild?" she asked when she returned.

"No, only in wildlife parks."

"Well, if you look up in that big tree near the toilets, the one lit up by the street lamp, you'll see one sitting in the cleft of a branch, looking down at you."

I stopped undressing, pulled my top back over my head and ran across to the toilet block. Sure enough, there was a koala staring down at me, blinking in the light. My first wild koala! The next morning, I was disappointed to find that he had decided not to stay the night.

Radio 4HI was is Esmond Street and we walked around there at nine o'clock. We didn't
know what time the office would open, but we thought that would be a reasonable time. A young man in shorts

and T-shirt was opening the door as we arrived.

"Good morning, ladies," he greeted us cheerfully. "What can we do for you today?"

"We have a story. We are looking for two men who have disappeared and we thought perhaps you could help us get the word out around these parts," Emma replied.

"Well, we'll see what we can do. Come in."

He led us in to the tiny office, behind which was a big window, revealing the broadcasting area. A large man with a short beard and tidy moustache was lounging in his chair, eyes closed, as he bobbed his head up and down to the music.

"That's Barry. He's the one who'll put the message out over the air for you," the young man who had introduced himself as Martin, informed us. "He doesn't come off air for another couple of hours, so I'll take down the details if you like and, if he wants to interview you later, he'll give you a call. How does that sound?"

"Fine," I replied, knowing we were completely in their hands.

We sat down with him for about twenty minutes and told him about Jayden and David being missing, how it was totally out of character and that his wife and a friend

74

of David's wife were here in Emerald searching for them. We stressed that we would like to hear from anyone who had spoken to them and, particularly, anyone who had seen them after they left Emerald. I made sure to mention how upset his wife and two beautiful daughters were that their husband and father were ten days overdue from a trip. Emma pointed out that Jayden was an experienced camper and it was totally out of character for him not to make contact. I added that, as their fossicking licence ran until 15 August, they might have come back to the area and we were hoping someone had seen or spoken to them towards the end of July.

We returned to the campervan and started writing our phone number, as well as that of 4HI, on the bottom of the photo, and the word "Missing" along the top.

"We should probably get some proper posters printed," I suggested. "We are not going to have enough of these photos anyway."

"That sounds like a job for you!" Emma declared. "I'm going down to the pub a bit later to talk to the bartender and some of the regulars."

I found a printer and returned later with four hundred posters showing the photo of Jayden and David with the slide-on camper and 'Missing' in big letters above it. Underneath I put the phone number for the police as well as my mobile number.

'Any news from the pub?" I asked Emma, hopefully.

"Nothing useful. A couple of the men thought they might have seen them in there, but they couldn't be sure. They hadn't spoken to them, at any rate, so that wasn't much help."

She sat down at the table and I prepared a couple of sandwiches. We spent the afternoon putting up posters all over town.

Martin had done a good job of taking down the details of our missing men and Barry had the story down pat when he rang me. He put the story out on the radio that afternoon and again the next morning. Four people came forward to say that they had seen either Jayden or David. One man said he had seen them in town on the seventeenth of July (he was sure of the date because it was his wife's birthday on the eighteenth and he had been in the newsagent buying her a card when they walked in and bought a newspaper) and a woman said she was sure she saw David at the supermarket around that time. They hadn't spoken to them and couldn't add anything further. Martin said a woman who worked at the caravan park on the other side of town to where we were staying, was able to confirm that they had stayed there from fifteenth of July to the nineteenth. We took her name, Julie, so that we could speak with her further. The last caller was Ray, who said he saw them fossicking down by the river and had spoken with them. This was on the nineteenth of July and they told him they hadn't had much luck, only finding a couple of very small emeralds. They had told him that they were going to head over to Sapphire and try their luck there.

We drove over to the caravan park where Julie worked, which was very similar to where we were staying. Julie was in the office and we introduced ourselves and explained why we were there. She was middle-aged with a welcoming smile and dark blonde hair pulled back into a ponytail. She apologised that she didn't have much more to add to what she had already told Barry at the radio station.

"They stayed here for four nights, but I didn't see much of them. They were very self-contained and no trouble. When they checked out on the nineteenth of July, I asked them where they were heading (I usually ask everyone that, just being friendly) and I remember they said they were going to Rubyvale and Sapphire. That's it, I'm afraid," she said.

77

"It is helpful, Julie, thank you. We know there is no point staying in Emerald any longer, we need to move on. I expect they would have stayed here again if they had returned this way."

"Yes, they might have done. You never can tell with these campers! Anyway, I hope you find them soon."

Tracking down Ray proved a little more difficult. He had given his address and phone number to Barry and we drove to the neat, fibro house on the edge of town. Painted a light green, it looked well maintained with a small front garden consisting of a tidy lawn with a few shrubs around the perimeter. There was no response from our knock, so we tried the neighbours on either side. One thought he had probably gone to the supermarket, the other sure that he had gone fossicking.

"Goes for days at a time, Ray does. He could be at Sapphire or anywhere, really."

A quick look around the side of the house revealed the absence of his caravan, so it seemed he might well have gone away. I rang the mobile number he had left with Barry.

"You just caught me," he said when he answered. "I'm at the garage, filling up with petrol, before heading off. I'll swing back by the house in about five minutes."

Ray pulled slowly into his driveway shortly afterwards and climbed out of his vehicle. Behind it was a small, older-style caravan. Ray was a man of about seventy, slim with grey, wispy hair and lively, grey eyes. He opened the front door to the house and invited us to follow him inside.

"Cup of coffee?" he inquired as we sat at the wooden table. "No milk, I'm afraid."

"No thanks," Emma replied. "We won't hold you up, Ray. We wanted to know if there is anything more you can tell us about our missing men."

Ray scratched his chin.

"I don't think so. I saw them fossicking down at the creek and stopped to chat for a few minutes. They asked me if I thought they had much chance of finding a big emerald at that spot and I laughed. No-one's found a big one for a while, I told them, but that's not to say one couldn't have been uncovered by the last rains. They said they had found a couple of very small ones and showed them to me. I told them they weren't worth much but to keep trying. They said they were going to try for sapphires in Sapphire and I wished them luck. That's about it. They seemed well set up and one of them

79

looked as if he knew what he was doing."

"That would be Jayden, my husband," Emma said.

"David's a city boy," I added.

"Well, I can't think what's happened to them. How long have they been missing?"

"They were due home around the fourth of August, so ten days," I told him.

"That's not a long while to be overdue in the outback. I wouldn't worry too much; I'm sure they'll turn up soon."

"It's been longer than that since we've heard from them," I told him.

"Well, unless they've run off, something must have happened," Ray said.

"That's why we are out looking for them," I explained. "I don't know what chance we have of finding them, but we are going to try. The police are looking too, but so far they haven't found anything."

"Well, I wish you luck. If I see them on my travels, I'll make sure they get in touch. I'm heading further west."

We thanked him for coming back to talk to us and returned to the caravan park.

During my usual evening chat with Mike, he picked

up on my disappointment.

"It was a great idea, Anna. Also, it's too soon to say that nothing will come from the call out on the radio. Sometimes people are away and other people mention it in conversation days later and it jogs their memory. Don't give up hope yet."

Sandra sounded disappointed too.

"I was so hoping you would have learned something, Anna. I ring the police every day, but it's always the same answer. 'We'll be in touch as soon as we hear anything Mrs Pearson.'

"We're getting closer, Sandra. We know that David and Jayden were here and tomorrow we are going to Sapphire. That's another place they might have called in at again on their way home. Keep your chin up, my friend. I'm sure we'll find something out soon."

Next morning, we were back on the road, heading for Sapphire, only a short drive away. I had spoken to Barry before we left and he promised to put the story over the air a few more times and to contact us straight away if he received any more calls in response.

Chapter Nine
On Track

The sun had a bite in it by the time we pulled into a caravan park at Sapphire. I was feeling weary; I hadn't slept well the night before, conscious of Emma lying beside me and missing Mike. I hoped he wasn't so busy at work that he had forgotten to miss me!

The owner of the caravan park didn't recognise the photo of David and Jayden so we split up and talked to as many people as we could, asking shops to put up our 'missing' poster and taping a few posters to telegraph poles. We met up again at a café in the main street, where we had coffee and a sandwich and discussed our morning. Neither of us had spoken to anyone who recognised our boys. It was depressing. Queensland is vast and we were trying to find two men, who could be almost anywhere. It was like looking for two needles in a haystack and hoping that we would find them together.

"If we can't find anyone here who remembers them, where are we going to go next?" I asked Emma as I bit into my sandwich.

"Well, Rubyvale first, obviously. That's not very far away. Then we have to decide if we go further north or turn west. You have to remember that they were only planning to be away for three weeks, and we know they went as far as Longreach. Then they were probably thinking about heading for home. The police have concentrated their efforts around Longreach but, so far, they haven't come up with anything, which makes me think they must have gone further north or west.

"For all we know, they may have stopped around here again on their return journey," I suggested.

"True. They can't have gone very far or one of their credit cards would have been used for petrol. If they were here recently, I think someone is going to remember seeing them. We have to ask a whole lot more questions."

I knew Emma was right, but I was discouraged by our lack of results. I knew I needed to shake myself out of this and focus on the job at hand.

"Right," I declared as I drained the last of my coffee. "Let's see what we can find out this afternoon.

We elected to stay together and drive around some of the prospecting sites.

"Who knows? We might even stumble across our guys, still busy prospecting and unaware of the time that has passed."

"Fat chance," Emma mumbled under her breath.

By the end of the day, we had spoken to two people who remembered seeing David and Jayden. The first was a prospector, a middle-aged man, short, rotund and looking like he was in need of a bath. He was helpful, in that he took a good look at the flyer we showed him before saying that yes, he did remember these two men. They had passed the time of day with him about a month ago, but he couldn't tell us much else. It was the vehicle he remembered more than David and Jayden, saying he had admired their set-up. He told us he came to Sapphire for a couple of months every winter and he showed us a few small sapphires which he had found.

The other person who remembered seeing them was the owner of the petrol station, Jim Dawson. He was able to tell us that David and Jayden had bought fuel from him and that he had talked to them for quite a while. He said that the boys were talking about leaving the gem fields and heading for Longreach. The shorter of the two men (Jayden) was telling the other man that they were never going to find any worthwhile gems, so David might as well more of Queensland and Longreach and Winton seemed to be the ultimate destination.

"You hadn't heard that these men are missing?" I asked.

"No, can't say I have. Not that it would have made any difference, I didn't have anything to tell anyone."

"What about them going on to Longreach?"

"People talk about a lot of things," he replied with a shrug. "Doesn't mean they are going to do them. It seemed to me that maybe they were just talking."

"Can you give us the date that they were here?" Emma asked.

Jim scratched his beard for a moment.

"I remember the shorter of the two paid for the fuel. I think he paid by credit card. You could have a look through the receipts if you like."

It was fortunate that Jayden had paid, because Emma knew his credit card number and I had no idea of David's. I made a mental note to ask Sandra for David's credit card number when I spoke to her next, in case we needed it later.

"Here it is!" Emma exclaimed after a few minutes. "Nineteenth of July."

We thanked Jim profusely and headed back to the caravan park. I wasn't sure that it helped us to know that

Jayden had bought petrol on nineteenth of July when we already knew that David had rung Sandra from Longreach on the thirtieth. Still, I supposed any information was helpful. At least Jim had informed us that Winton could have been their final destination.

I was delighted to see a group of kangaroos on the grass in front of the caravans – a mother, father and baby and four others a little further away. I watched, fascinated, as the baby put himself back into mum's pouch. It was one thing seeing kangaroos in the paddocks from the car, but to see them close up, watching them chew and scratch themselves, was special. Although I had lived in Australia for a large part of my life, there aren't any kangaroos running around in Sydney, so I had seen very few.

"We might as well drive on to Rubyvale now," Emma declared. "I'll tell these people we have decided not to stay the night after all. Hopefully they won't charge us anything, knowing why we are here."

"I think we should stay here longer. We've found two people who saw the boys. Maybe we'll find some more if we keep asking."

"I guess so. Okay, we'll give it another day."

We might as well have headed straight for Rubyvale

because, despite asking twenty or thirty people, no-one was able to give us any information.

"Is it going to rain?" I asked, looking up at the sky, as we returned to the caravan park. Black clouds had rolled in, blocking the sun.

"It would be unusual for this time of year, but it definitely looks like it."

A few minutes later there was a crack of thunder and a lightening flash. We retreated inside and watched as large drops of water fell to the ground. They were swiftly followed by a deluge of rain that lasted all night, hammering on the roof of the campervan and disturbing my efforts to sleep.

Rubyvale was a mere seven kilometres away and we arrived shortly after eight o'clock in the morning. The rain had followed us. At the caravan park, the man who took our money had no recollection of seeing our missing men and, frankly, wasn't very interested. He did agree to let us put up a poster, which I stuck on the window of his cabin, in full view of anyone booking in or out.

Barry, from the radio station in Emerald, rang a couple of hours later, to give me the latest update on his call-outs over the air for information on Jayden and David. He told me he had received five calls, all saying they remembered seeing the men or their camper in the area, but all when they would have been heading out. No-one had seen them in recent days. I took down their names and phone numbers and said I would speak to them, but I knew it was going to be an exercise in thanking them for calling in, rather than gleaning anything useful. I stayed in the caravan to make the calls, whilst Emma headed out with some posters.

"How did you go with the phone calls?" she asked on her return.

"As we expected. They were all very helpful and told me where they had seen David or Jayden, but there are no recent sightings."

I showed her the list I had made of where our men had been seen and she glanced at it briefly.

"How about you? Have you found anyone who has seen them?"

"Not yet, but I'll keep trying."

"I'll come and help you now. We can grab a sandwich at a café; that's definitely a good place to start."

The girl serving in the café where we ate took a good

look at the photo but couldn't remember seeing them. She kindly showed it to a couple of locals sitting on bar stools, but they too shook their heads. We left a poster with her to put up in the window and went looking for some prospectors. They were still hard at work, even in the rain. We spent the afternoon showing the photo to prospectors spread out around the area, trying not to get it wet, but no-one remembered seeing either of the boys.

That night we had a decision to make. Where were we going to go from Rubyvale? We knew the boys had made it to Longreach. Was it likely they were still in that area or would they have moved on long ago?

"What do you think the chances are that they headed further north?" I asked Emma as we drank a cold beer in the caravan.

"Knowing Jayden, pretty good I'd say. He likes to keep moving and he likes driving up the coast. He likes going to Cooktown too."

"But they would have needed petrol. The police said their credit cards hadn't been used since the first of August."

"Jayden carries quite a lot of cash with him, usually. David probably had some too."

"They could have paid cash, I suppose."

We sipped our beers, trying to work out the best place to head for next.

"Trouble is," she added, after a few minutes, "if they had gone up the coast road and something had happened there would be plenty of people to give them a hand. They wouldn't have been out of touch all this time."

"We've been looking for five days now. When I spoke to Sandra tonight, she sounded very down. She says the thought that we are out here trying to find them is the only thing keeping her going."

I pulled out the map and we mulled over it together.

"They could be almost anywhere," I said after a while, pushing the map away. "We might as well put a pin in it."

Emma picked up the map and pointed. "I reckon they must have gone up the Great Inland Way; it's shorter," Emma decided. "It would be about a twelve-hour trip from Winton, through Hughenden to Cooktown. Then I think Jayden would have planned to come back from Cooktown via the Pacific Coast Way. Look, we can pick up the Great Inland Way from Capella, here," she pointed.

I peered at the map.

"There will be lots of road trains using that road, so you'll have to be on your toes, Anna. They stop for nothing and no-one! Couldn't, even if they wanted to!"

"Road trains are those big trucks with several semi-trailers behind them, aren't they?"

"Yes. They can weigh up to two hundred tonnes and they drive fast. If you see dust coming your way, you need to move over and give him plenty of room, 'cause they don't even slow down."

"Okay," I said, with more confidence than I felt. "But there aren't many towns along there, are there? How are we going to find out anything?"

"We can only keep our eyes peeled, in case they are stranded off the road. We can ask people at Capella," she said, pointing, "Claremont, here and Belyando Crossing. If we can find even one person who has seen them along that route, we'll know we are on the right track."

"That's true. It would be good to know we are going the right way." I wiped the drops of sweat from my forehead with a tissue. The rain had stopped as suddenly as it had started and it was going to be a hot one today. "I don't want to be a pessimist, but what if no-one has seen them along that route?"

"I think we keep going as far as Cairns and ask around there. I can't think of anything else to do, unless the police or someone else finds them in the meantime."

"I think we should go to Longreach and Winton first. After all, we know they were in that area. If they called from Longreach on July thirtieth, I can't see why they would try to get to Cooktown if they were going to be home in Sydney by fourth of August. It doesn't make sense to me."

"Well, there's not much in Longreach and Winton. You'd see everything in two or three days. The police have searched all that area. Jayden loves going to Cooktown, not that there's much there either. He likes that drive, I think. They could have planned to have a quick look around and then come straight through to Sydney, and make it home by the fourth."

"I still think we should talk to people around Longreach and Winton. How long will it take us to get to Longreach?"

Emma sighed and I reminded myself that it was her husband with David and that, by now, she must be worried about him. She studied the map.

"About four hours."

"I'm sorry, Emma. I know this must be so hard for

you."

"Ah well. What to do, eh? We'll keep looking and hope that someone finds them. Alright, if you want to try Longreach and Winton first, we'll do it."

When I came back from the toilet block some time during the night, I was sure I could hear Emma crying. I climbed over her on to my side of the bed and put an arm around her. She blew her nose loudly and soon we both fell asleep.

Chapter Ten
A Shocking Find

We put some more posters up around Rubyvale the next day, spoke to a few more people and then, not having had any success, hit the road to Longreach. If we were lucky enough to find someone there who had spoken to either of the boys, they might be able to give us some idea where they were headed and, hopefully, save us a trip to Cairns!

Longreach and Winton were an education for me. The dust, the dirt and the tourists! People flocked from all over the world to see the dinosaur footprints and museum at Winton. The rain hadn't been sufficient to cause any flooding, fortunately, but the sun was hot now and the combination of rain and sun meant it was extremely humid. The weather forecast was for thirty-one degrees today and it felt like it. I could feel the sweat trickling down my neck and back as I sipped on one of the bottles of water Emma always insisted that we have with us. I was glad of my hat to keep the sun off my face and neck.

Tourists stopped at Longreach to visit the Stockman's Hall of Fame and the Qantas Museum. I would have liked to see them myself, since we were there, but I knew we needed to keep talking to people to see if they had seen our boys, so I only went as far as the entrances, to talk to the staff. Longreach, the largest town in Central Queensland, was much larger than I had envisaged, flat with lots of shops and cafes. With so many tourists visiting each day, I wasn't surprised that no-one remembered seeing David or Jayden. It was the same at the Australian Age of Dinosaurs Museum at Winton. Emma insisted that I see the dinosaur footprints at the Dinosaur Stampede National Monument in Lake Quarry, whilst we were there. She said it would be such a waste to have come so far and not see such a great part of Australian history. It turned out to be an amazing experience and I was so glad not to have missed it. The footprints were massive and there were so many of them, over three thousand, I was told. They looked as if they had been made recently, not all those years ago. I could almost imagine the dinosaurs stampeding through this place, a wild and frightening vision. It was something I would always remember and I was pleased to think of David having visited here. I am sure he would have had the same reaction as me.

Emma had been busy speaking to people in my

absence, but not to any avail. We spent the night at Winton and then, having learned nothing new, retraced our footsteps, heading for Capella. I was glad that Emma didn't say 'I told you so.' She hadn't been kidding about the road trains, either. The first time I saw one, it was like a huge train bearing down on us at speed.

"Is this a road train coming towards us, Emma?"

Emma checked through the windscreen. "Sure is. Slow down and pull over as far as you can."

I watched with dread and fascination as tonnes of metal raced towards us. It barely slowed and I found myself coming almost to a stop and putting two wheels off the road. The wind as the road train passed, rocked us.

"Wow!" I said.

"It's wow alright. Usually, they leave enough room for you to stay on the road, but it's a good idea to slow down. You did alright. Next time you'll know what to expect."

We found a parking spot in the street with the pole murals relating to the Light Horse Emu Plume Project at Capella. The story goes that, during the Great Shearers' Strike of 1891, some troopers hunted down emus when things were quiet on their long patrols and then pulled out the feathers, which they placed in their hat band. Later, as recognition of their service during the shearers' strike, the Queensland Government made it official that they could wear emu plumes in their hats as part of their uniform.

We spent the next couple of hours talking to shop owners and locals, but we couldn't find anyone who had seen David or Jayden. I was very glad of my long-sleeved shirt and hat as the sun was beating down mercilessly, so I only stayed for a quick look at the memorial, depicting a soldier and his horse. When I complained to Emma about the heat, she said it wasn't very hot, not for central Queensland, where in summer the temperature usually stays around forty degrees. It was hot enough for me.

We continued on to Clermont, another fifty or so kilometres north. Clermont was quite a revelation. After the dust, dirt and barrenness of the gem-prospecting towns, Clermont was like an oasis, green and pleasant. There were cattle and sheep in lush paddocks as well as fields of grain crops. We booked into a caravan park for the night and I took our washing to the laundrette. Whilst I waited for the machine to go through its cycle, I read some information on the town. Clermont was built on the banks of Hood's Lagoon where it existed happily for fifty years as a gold-prospecting town. In 1916 a huge flood swept through the town causing enormous destruction and taking the lives of sixty-five people. Three pianos were left wedged in the trees after the flood, and today there is still one piano lodged high up in a tree, as a reminder of this tragedy. We had seen it driving in. Monuments to honour those killed have been erected around Hood's Lagoon. Following the flood, the town was moved to higher ground. Today, murals can be seen painted on old railway carriages, depicting the main activities of the area.

I walked into the shops close to the laundrette and spoke to several people, none of whom had any news for me. I put up a few posters, collected our clean clothes and returned to the caravan park. Emma had been to the pubs and talked to several locals and visitors, none of whom had seen David or Jayden. Although it was frustrating when people said they hadn't seen Jayden or David, we also had plenty of laughs. A few men made jokes about what could have happened to our boys, perhaps thinking we were exaggerating the situation. "Might have been attacked by a kangaroo," one middle-aged drinker suggested. "Probably bitten by a large brown snake when he reached down to pick up a sapphire," another offered. Not so funny, that one. "Run off with a couple of country sheilas," or "Had to get that far away from his missus?" were heard more than once. Mostly people were genuinely concerned and wished they could be more helpful.

When I spoke to Mike that evening, he said he had called in on Sandra and the girls on the way home and they were as well as could be expected. Avril wanted to know when I was going to find her daddy, Bethany needed him to put the head back on one of her dolls and Sandra asked him to look at a dripping tap in the ensuite. He said he had explained to Avril that I was out looking for her daddy and he soon re-attached the head on Bethany's doll. Promising to go over for lunch on Sunday and to change the tap washer, he had only been home for a few minutes. I told him how green and fresh it was in Clermont and about the piano in the tree. I managed to make Sandra laugh a few minutes later when I rang her and told her the same story.

"Look it up on the internet – you won't believe it!"

"I will. I'll show the girls too. I can tell them that is where their daddy was." She sighed. "I do hope you can find them soon, Anna. I'm going crazy here wondering what has happened to David."

"I know you must be, Sandra. We are trying. It's very hard to know where to look, but we will keep talking to people. We've put up a lot of posters, so even when we leave these towns, travellers from all sorts of places will see them."

"Thanks Anna. It must be hard for you too, so far away from Mike and camping too! How's that going?"

"It's definitely not my thing, Sandra! I hate having to go to the ablutions blocks for showers and the toilet. Give me an ensuite any day! Sharing a bed with Emma isn't exactly a highlight either, although even that's not too bad."

"I do appreciate what you are doing. It's just....well, you know, it's so awful. It's hard trying to be brave for the girls."

"Do they ask after their daddy?"

"Not often, thank goodness, but they have their moments. Then they don't understand why he hasn't phoned them in so long."

"Maybe you could tell them that he rang during the

night, when they were asleep?"

"I suppose I could, but I don't want to start lying to them."

"Keep thinking about how great it will be when you see him again, Sandra. He will turn up eventually."

"I hope you're right, Anna. Anyway, sleep well and, who knows, tomorrow may be the day!"

It was a throw-away line, but it turned out to be prophetic.

We spent the morning talking to people and putting up more posters and had returned to the caravan for a cup of tea. I was waiting for the kettle to boil when Emma's phone rang.

"Yes, this is Mrs Watson. Where am I? Clermont. Yes, I suppose we could. Do you have some news on my husband, Jayden? No detective, I'm not alone, Anna Davies is here with me. We're about to have a cup of tea. Okay, we'll come now."

"What is it?"

"That was the police station, here at Clermont. They want us to go in to the police station. I think they have some news about Jayden and David, but they won't tell me over the phone."

I switched off the kettle and we drove straight to the police station. A young policewoman showed us into a small room and no sooner had she left than a middle-aged Senior Sergeant entered.

"Mrs Watson?"

"Yes," Emma replied.

"And you are?" he said, turning to me.

"I'm Anna Davies. David Pearson's wife is my best friend. That's why I'm here with Emma, trying to find them."

"I'm Sergeant Barry Armstrong. Thank you for coming in. I've had a phone call from a Detective John Brady and, I'm very sorry to tell you this Mrs Watson, but a body has been found in Blackdown National Park and we have reason to believe it may be your husband."

"NO......NO........that can't be right. No, there must be some mistake! Not my Jayden! You must have the wrong person."

"He hasn't been formally identified yet, of course, but he was found next to his slide-on camper, with his phone and wallet and the photo on his Driver's Licence leads us to believe it is Jayden. I'm very sorry."

I put my arm around Emma's shoulders.

"It can't be Jayden," she said, turning to look at me,

her eyes wide with shock. "This can't be true!"

"Do you have any news on David Pearson? Is David dead too?" I asked the Sergeant.

"No, we don't know where David is. He wasn't at the scene of the crime. I don't have all the details, but Detective John Brady from Rockhampton Police Station is in charge of this case and he would like to speak with you." He dialled a number and passed the phone to Emma.

"You speak to him, Anna," Emma said and I took the phone from her.

Detective John Brady said he had been given Emma's number by the police in Sydney. Two men had come across Jayden's slide-on camper in Blackdown Tableland National Park, about one hundred and eighty kilometres east of Rockhampton. It was in rugged bushland and they pulled up next to it, to see if they needed any assistance. To their shock, they found a body lying on the ground behind it. They said it was obvious that the man had been dead for some time and there was no sign of anyone else near the vehicle. They checked his pockets to find his wallet with his Driver's Licence, giving his name and address, along with a mobile phone. They reported that he appeared to have been in the middle of changing a tyre when he died. There was a flat tyre behind the vehicle, as well as a wheel brace, which had dried blood on it. They walked around for a while, calling out, to see if anyone else was alive, as they could see another mobile phone on the passenger's side of the dashboard. They couldn't get any mobile phone coverage out there, so they had to drive back to town to report finding a dead man. The police soon had a contingent of men combing the area around where the body was found. The two men who had made the discovery drove back to the scene and handed the phone and wallet to the police. Detective Brady said he was very sorry, but they had good reason to believe that the dead man was her husband, Jayden."

"I see."

"Would you mind asking Mrs Watson if she knows the password to unlock Mr Watson's phone?"

Emma gave me the pin number and Detective Brady said they had been in touch with Sandra for David's password, as they believe the other phone found in the vehicle probably belonged to him. Then he gave me his phone number, saying to contact him again if we had any questions when we had digested the information.

"Oh, Emma," I said as I put the phone down on the table. "I'm so, so sorry. This is so awful."

We made our way out of the police station and back to the campervan.

"I can't believe it. Not Jayden. He can't be dead, he can't be." She sat down and put her head in her hands. I leaned against her, as her heart-rending sobs filled the campervan. I couldn't imagine how I would feel if it was Mike. Mike! Thank goodness he had been too busy at work to go on this trip with David. It could have been him lost or, worse, dead! I wondered if Sandra had been given the news yet. I would have to ring her. What was I going to say? How could I convince her that, somehow, David is still alive. I didn't even know that myself. If he is alive, where is he?

I hugged Emma as she cried. For half-an-hour she moaned and sobbed and I ached for her. Eventually she stopped and looked up at me with bloodshot eyes, her face blotchy. She blew her nose loudly on the tissue I handed to her.

"What are we going to do now?"

"I don't know, Emma. I think I should make us a cup of tea and then we can think about it."

As we drank our tea, I could see the disbelief on

Emma's face. Such a shock! I was finding it hard to take it in myself.

"I wonder where David is?" I asked. "Do you think the police will find his body too, somewhere nearby?"

"It seems likely. Since he wasn't in the car, he must have tried to make a run for it. Why would anyone want to kill them, Anna? Do you think they could have found some valuable gemstones?"

"Who knows? I'm sure David, at least, would have happily handed them over rather than risk being killed."

"Jayden wouldn't have wanted to die for them either. Oh, my poor Jayden. How I am going to miss him!"

"I can't believe it either, Emma. It's like some dreadful nightmare. I know you hear about people being shot or stabbed on the news, but you never think it is going to happen to someone you know."

"Didn't you say you had been involved in solving mysteries over the years? Did any of those involve murders?"

Emma hadn't asked anything about my past on the drive up, so I hadn't mentioned it again.

"Yes, unfortunately, they all involved deaths or murders. It doesn't make it any easier though, especially when it's your husband - and when the husband of my best friend could be involved, too."

"We have to decide our next move, but sometime later I'd like you to tell me about them."

"Okay. As you say, we have to decide what we are going to do next. I'm sure you want to see Jayden."

Emma let out a big sob. "Yes."

"They'll need you to identify him, anyway."

Another big sob. I grabbed the map and spread it out on the table. "Let's see where that National Park is from here."

We found Blackdown Tableland National Park, about one hundred and seventy-five kilometres from Clermont.

"Do you have any idea why they would be there? Did you and Jayden go there before?" I asked.

"No, I can't remember going there. I guess they were out and about enjoying the bush."

I did some googling on my phone.

"It's not a very large National Park, but it does have some Aboriginal paintings. Maybe Jayden wanted to show them to David. I don't expect he has ever seen any and it wouldn't have been far to go."

"I guess."

"I'll ring Detective Brady back and find out when and

where you can see Jayden."

Emma nodded.

More in charge of my senses now, I dialled Detective Brady's number. He told me that Jayden was being taken to Rockhampton, as was the vehicle. Forensics would go all over the camper in Rockhampton, looking for fingerprints and any clue as to Jayden's killer. I said we would make our way there, so that Emma could identify him.

"It won't be a facial identification, as I'm sure you can understand. Too much time has passed. We need her to identify some of his clothing, his watch, that kind of thing. I don't suppose her husband had any identifying marks on him?

"Emma, does Jayden have any identifying mark on his body?"

"Yes, he had a small tattoo on the inside of his wrist. It's the name of his son, Peter, who died."

It hadn't occurred to me that Jayden would be unrecognisable by now. The thought made me feel nauseous and I was quiet for a minute or two.

"Are you pretty sure it's Jayden?" I asked.

"Yes, Mrs Davies, I'm sorry, but we are. He had his wallet and his Driver's Licence in his pocket."

I relayed Emma's message about the tattoo.

"Does Mrs Watson know the name of his dentist?"

"Emma, do you know the name of Jayden's dentist? They want to confirm his dental records."

"Er....yes, of course. It's Rob Walker. Jayden has been going to him for years. Let me find my phone and I'll give you his phone number."

"What about David? Do you have any idea where he is?" I asked, whilst she looked.

"We haven't found him yet, Mrs Davies. We still have men out looking for him."

Emma passed me her phone and I read out the phone number for Rob Walker.

"Thanks, we'll contact Mr Walker and get Jayden's dental records."

"What do you think happened, detective?"

"At this stage, we don't know, Mrs Davies. It looks as if he was shot. Do you know if David had a gun with him?"

"David? No way! He's a city boy, he wouldn't have a gun," I replied, incredulously.

"What about Jayden? Would he have had a gun with him?"

I asked Emma if Jayden might have been carrying a

gun. She shook her head in the negative.

"No, he didn't have one either."

"You see, one of my thoughts is that maybe they had an argument and David shot Jayden."

The suggestion stunned me for a minute, before the words rushed out. "You can't be serious! David isn't like that. There is no way he would have shot Jayden."

"Well, that's only one line of thought. We're pretty sure we can rule out suicide, but the post-mortem will confirm that."

"I know David would never shoot anyone, Detective. Besides, if he had shot him, he would have taken the vehicle. He wouldn't walk away when he's in the middle of nowhere," I pointed out, reasonably.

"He might have panicked. Run off in shock. We're looking at every angle, Mrs Davies, so there's no need to get upset. The other possibility is that they ran into foul play. Maybe they picked up a hiker. David might have managed to get away and hide. Or maybe the killer took him with him - or them - we don't know. Forensics will have a good look around the area and let us know if there was another vehicle or footprints. I'll keep you informed. In the meantime, if you can make your way to Rockhampton, the sooner we can arrange for Mrs

Watson to identify her husband, the better."

I could see Emma was in deep shock. I washed our cups and started to pack up the campervan. It would be up to me now to step up.

"I want to see where Jayden died," Emma stated when I had finished. "It's sort of on the way, anyway."

I didn't argue, knowing she had made up her mind and it was something she needed to do. We could have gone after she had seen Jayden, but since it was on the way, it made sense to do it now. It would give the police more time to find something out.

"I have to ring Sandra before we go. Mike too."

Emma went back to staring into the distance.

"Sandra. You've heard about Jayden?"

"Yes, the police rang. It's awful. I can't believe he's dead. I'm so worried about David. Do you think he is dead too, Anna?"

"No, Sandra, I don't. You shouldn't think like that either. We have to be positive. The fact he hasn't been found anywhere near the vehicle makes me think he got away from the killer."

"But it's been so long, Anna. It's two weeks since they

were due home and the police said Jayden had been dead for quite a while. So where is David? How could he not have got in touch with us in all this time? He must be dead, Anna. He must be. If he was alive, he would have contacted me somehow."

"Perhaps when they look at Jayden and David's phones there will be something there to give them a clue." "

"Maybe, but they've been tracking them anyway. Anna, I'm going mad here. The girls don't understand why I can't stop crying. I've told them I have a tummy ache but that won't fool them for long."

"I wish I was there for you, Sandra."

"No, you have to keep looking for him, Anna! Only you will keep looking until he is found. I need you to do this for me."

"Okay, Sandra. I promise I'll keep looking. You have to promise me you will try not to think the worse yet."

"I do," she sobbed. "I'll try not to, but it's so hard, this not knowing. If it's bad news though, I don't want to know. I'd rather keep on hoping. At least Mum and Dad arrived today. They are going to stay with me until David is found."

"That's good, Sandra. They can help you take care of

the girls and make sure you eat."

She cried for a while and I tried to make soothing noises over the phone. After a while she pulled herself together.

"I must let you go, Anna. Go and find David for me, please."

"I'll try. I should mention that the police asked if David had a gun."

"A gun? David? No, of course he didn't. Why would they ask that?

"One theory was that maybe David and Jayden had an argument and David shot Jayden."

"No, you know he didn't, Anna! David's isn't aggressive. How could they think that?"

"Well, they don't know him like we do, but I told them that there was no way David could shoot anyone. He said they were looking at all angles. I'm pretty sure they've ruled out suicide."

"Why wouldn't David have taken the vehicle if he's still alive? It doesn't make sense to leave it there."

"That's what I said! They don't know, Sandra. It's one of the things they are investigating. We are going to drive to the Blackdown National Park now. Emma wants to see where Jayden was found. Then we are going to Rockhampton, so that she can identify him from his clothing, etc; it's been too long since he died for a proper identification. It won't be easy for her. I'll ring you when we know for sure that it is Jayden, but everything fits. They have his wallet, his Driver's Licence, the vehicle...."

"Okay. Please be careful, Anna. There is a killer out there and I don't want anything to happen to you."

"I will be. Speak to you soon. Say hi to the girls for me. Love you."

Mike wasn't quite as keen for me to stay in Queensland.

"Come home now, darling. Let the police look for David. It's too dangerous now, with a killer running around."

"I'd like to, Mike, honestly I would, but how can I tell Sandra I have given up whilst David is still missing? Besides, Emma needs me at the moment. We have to drive to Rockhampton so that she can identify Jayden's clothing and things. I don't think there is much I can do, but I need to support Emma and I can't have Sandra thinking that I have given up. Besides, what are the chances of us running into the killer? We can't even find

David."

He gave one of his exasperated sighs, but I knew he could see my point.

"Be careful. Don't take any chances. At the first hint of danger, run. Let the police deal with it. Agreed?"

"Definitely. Love you."

"Love you too. Can't wait to have you home again."

Chapter Eleven
Emma's Nightmare

We arrived at Blackdown Tableland National Park a little over three hours later. Emma had hardly said a word the whole way, sitting quietly in the passenger seat, staring resolutely out of the window. I could only imagine the thoughts that were going through her head.

The road that led into the park was narrow and twisty. We knew that Jayden had been found off the four-wheel drive loop road. It was well sign-posted and we drove for a while, looking into the bush, searching for Jayden's vehicle. It wasn't hard to find - the police had the area cordoned off and signs out. We parked at the side of the road and walked as close to Jayden's vehicle as the tape would allow. We couldn't get close to where Jayden was found. I was glad that an ambulance had already taken him to Rockhampton. There were forensic people searching the vehicle, for fingerprints I presumed and, in the distance, I could see two policemen with dogs, scouring the bush. We walked further along the tape and could see the edge of an area marked out where Jayden's body would have been found. A tilt-tray vehicle was waiting for forensics to finish their preliminary search so that they could take the vehicle away. I wondered vaguely why they didn't drive it, but decided it was probably to avoid contamination. Whilst we waited, one of the dog handlers came back to near where we were standing and spoke to someone in plain clothes who appeared to be in charge. After speaking with the dog handler, the officer came across to us.

"Can I help you two ladies? This is a crime scene you know."

"I'm Emma Watson. It's my husband you found."

"My apologies, Mrs Watson. I know this must be very hard for you. I'm Detective Ross Grant. The ambulance has already left to take your husband's body to Rockhampton. I suggest you head over to Rockhampton. They'll need someone to identify him."

"Yes, we are on our way, but Emma wanted to see the place where her husband died."

Detective Grant nodded his understanding.

"We haven't found any trace of the other man. The dogs have had a good check around here, but they lose the scent a few yards from the vehicle. You can see there are tyre tracks from another vehicle," he pointed to some faint tracks. "It may be that Mr Pearson went in the other vehicle, either willingly or unwillingly. We found another phone on the dashboard, which appears to be his, so he left in a hurry."

"So, you think he could still be alive?" I asked hopefully.

"It's possible. There's no trace of him around here."

"It's been such a long while though," I said. "Where could he be all this time?"

"That's something we'll be looking at. In the meantime, we'll get the vehicle back to the yard and forensics can have a thorough look over it. I'm sorry for your loss, Mrs Watson," he added before walking over to the police car.

I ran after him. "Excuse me, Detective. Can I take David's phone back to his wife?"

"Not yet, I'm afraid. We'll hang on to it for now, let forensics look it over. You never know, there may be someone else's finger prints on it."

"I see. Thank you, detective."

I returned to where Emma was standing staring out in to the bush.

"Do you want to see anything else, Emma?"

"No, I don't think so. Not much to see, is there? I needed to see where he died. I thought maybe I'd feel some kind of connection, you know?"

"You didn't?"

"No, nothing. I hope it was quick and he didn't see it coming. He'd have liked to die out in the bush."

She took a final look around and climbed back into the passenger seat.

We drove to Rockhampton in a little under two-and-a-half hours. On the way I tried to get Emma talking again; it was unnerving, the way she sat so quietly, staring straight ahead.

"How long were you and Jayden married, Emma?"

"Um...fifteen years. It was a second marriage for us both."

"You don't have any children?"

"No, we didn't want them. I have a daughter from my first marriage, Angie, but Jayden and his first wife lost their son when he was only a few months old."

"How sad."

"It was. Jayden said he wasn't a healthy baby, he had problems from birth. His wife had some genetic disease, I forget what it was and they decided not to try for any more children."

"Have you rung Angie?"

"No. I should, I suppose. She's busy with her own

119

life. She has three young children, plus she works part-time. We don't see a lot of them since they moved to Port Macquarie."

"I'm sure she would want to be there for you now, Emma. You'll be glad of her support over the coming weeks."

When we reached Rockhampton, we went straight to Rockhampton Morgue. Emma introduced herself and asked to see her husband.

"That's not a good idea, Mrs Watson," a man who introduced himself as Ralph Manning, informed her. He had sympathetic brown eyes and I sensed a compassionate nature. I thought he was a good choice of person for this job. "Your husband has been dead for two to three weeks and, well, you understand the body naturally starts to break down after that time. He is not going to look like your husband. Then there are the animals in the bush. Trust me on this, you don't want to remember him as he is now. We have his wallet, his watch and mobile phone and some pieces of clothing, including his boots. Perhaps you could identify those for us?"

Close to tears, Emma conceded.

"I believe that your husband had a small tattoo on the inside of his wrist?"

"Yes, Peter."

"I'll show you the tattoo, but leave his face covered. Okay?"

"Okay."

"If you would wait here for a few minutes, I'll contact Detective Brady. I know he wants to be here when you view the items.

Detective Brady arrived within ten minutes and shook our hands.

"It's nice to meet you, Mrs Watson. I'm sorry it's under these circumstances. Thank you for coming here so quickly."

We were taken into a small room and an officer brought in Jayden's belongings. Emma sobbed quietly as she identified his watch and wallet. She sobbed louder when they showed her remnants of a blue and red check shirt and a pair of sturdy brown walking boots.

"Yes, they are Jayden's," she managed to say.

Then they took her to a small viewing window. In the room behind was a long table, with a body lying on it, covered with a sheet. A man in a white coat pulled the sheet across, revealing an arm, with the hand turned up.

On the wrist was tattooed a single word, Peter. Emma turned to Detective Brady.

"That's my Jayden, Detective," she managed to say.

"We'll confirm positively that it is your husband when the dental records are received, you understand."

"Yes, I understand," I heard Emma reply, her voice sounding hollow and resigned.

"We didn't learn anything new from their mobile phones and there has been no further activity on either of their credit cards. We think Jayden must have died not long after they left Longreach."

I hated myself for the relief I felt that it was definitely Jayden and not David who was dead.

As we prepared to leave, Detective Brady asked us what we intended to do now.

"We'll book in to a caravan park for tonight. Then it will depend on when you can release Jayden's body and the vehicle. We haven't made any plans past today," I explained.

Detective Brady recommended the caravan park on the outskirts of town and told us that he would keep us informed.

Emma was still quiet and it was getting late, so I made

dinner from our provisions so that we could eat sitting outside our campervan. I opened a couple of beers, as I thought they might help us to sleep. Whilst we ate, Emma asked me to tell her about the other mysteries I had been involved in over the years.

"Why don't I tell you about one each night; like a bedtime story? It will help to pass some time."

"Sounds good to me. Which one will it be tonight?"

"I'll start at the beginning. This story is about my time in Egypt. It all began when a man called Kareem Hazif walked into my office. I was in my thirties, working for a Federal Member of Parliament and he was seeking assistance to find his missing brother...."

Despite my bedtime story, or maybe because of it, neither of us slept well that night, tossing and turning until daybreak, when we were relieved to be able to get out of bed. I made breakfast and cleared up.

"Emma, I'm going to make some enquiries in Rockhampton whilst we are waiting. I'll see if anyone recognises David. I'll ring Barry at the radio station in Emerald too and tell him about Jayden. He can keep the story going and maybe, just maybe, someone will know where David is."

"You know he's dead too, don't you," she stated in a

flat voice.

"No, Emma, I don't know that and neither do you."

"Why else would no-one have seen him? If he were alive, he would have turned up somewhere by now."

"Normally, I'd agree with you, but I have a feeling David is still alive. I'm not sure if it is something I know, or something I want to believe at this point in time, but I'm not giving up on him. I can't sit here in the campervan waiting for the police to release Jayden and the vehicle. Do you want to stay or are you coming with me?"

I thought Emma was going to stay put, but after a couple of minutes she stood up and said she might as well come with me, it would be better than sitting and thinking. We spent the morning asking around. I had folded the picture of David and Jayden down the middle, so we only asked people if they had seen David. Not one person remembered seeing him. In the afternoon we went to a printer and he made some new posters for us; same wording but with a photo of David which Sandra had sent me, as well as a photo of the slide-on camper which Emma had provided. We spent a couple of hours putting them up. It was a long evening and eventually we took an early night and both slept much better than we had the previous night.

Over breakfast I carefully raised the subject of what we were going to do next.

"I have to arrange for Jayden to be taken home and then I have to arrange his funeral."

"I know, but I thought I might stay on here for a while."

"What are you going to do? You won't have a vehicle, unless you want me to leave this one with you. I suppose I could. Do you think you can manage on your own?"

"I think so. After all, I am woman! Seriously though, I've learned a lot from you since we left Sydney."

"Yes, I know, but there's a killer out there, somewhere. It's not safe for you to go looking on your own."

I knew Mike would agree with her and would want me to head for home, but I couldn't abandon David and Sandra.

We finished eating and I washed the dishes whilst Emma dried them.

"You know, I want Jayden's killer found. Once the funeral is over, there isn't going to be a great deal for me to do. I reckon I might come with you and help you look for David. I'm thinking I could take the campervan I borrowed back to Sydney and return it to my friend, leaving our outfit here. Then I could fly back and we could hit the road again."

"Would you really do that?" I felt relief rush through me. I might have sounded tough, but I knew I wasn't happy about driving around on my own, looking for David, knowing Jayden's killer was out there somewhere.

"Why don't you drive back with me? You could see Mike for a few days, talk to Sandra and then we could fly back to Rockhampton and head off again fresh. In the meantime, with a bit of luck, David might have turned up, or the police might have found the killer."

It sounded like an excellent plan to me and I knew I should go to Jayden's funeral. I was thrilled at the thought of going home to see Mike. Having a break from the campervan also delighted me; besides, I wanted to see Sandra and the girls. I knew Sandra was worried sick and worrying about me, as well, wasn't helping.

Emma spent most of the day arranging Jayden's funeral. She rang an undertaker near their home and he agreed to make the arrangements for Jayden's body to be collected from the morgue when it was released and returned to Sydney for the funeral. She looked on the undertaker's website and chose an order of service and some music. The undertaker said he would take care of the notice in the newspaper and that she could choose the coffin when she returned to Sydney. I suggested that maybe she should wait for confirmation of the dental records but Emma said there was no doubt already in her mind that Jayden was dead. Emma said it would take us fifteen or sixteen hours to drive the one thousand, four hundred kilometres back to Sydney.

Detective Brady rang around midday on Monday to advise that Jayden's body would be released the following morning. They would need to keep the slide-on camper for a few more days.

"What have you discovered?" Emma asked, putting her phone on speaker.

"First of all, the dental records have been received and there is no doubt I'm afraid, that the body is that of your husband, Jayden Watson."

Emma clenched her hands together but made no sound.

"The post-mortem revealed that Jayden died from a single shot to the head, from a 202 rifle, fired at close range. He would have died instantly. He hadn't been moved, so he died where he was found. The Sydney police have been in touch with Mrs Pearson and she has given them the contact details for David's brother, so that we can check his DNA against blood found on the wheel brace, which didn't belong to Jayden. As you know, there was evidence of another vehicle at the scene, but there is no way of knowing whether those tyre marks were made before or after Jayden's vehicle was parked there. No trace of David Pearson was found anywhere near the vehicle and the police dogs were unable to pick up his scent away from the crime scene. Our best guess is that he left in the killer's vehicle. Whether he was forced, or whether they were accomplices, we don't know."

"You may not know, detective, but I do," I interrupted. "I can assure you that David had nothing to do with Jayden's murder."

"Well, be that as it may, Mrs Davies, we are pretty sure that David left in the killer's vehicle. There were no fingerprints found on the vehicle, apart from those of Jayden and David."

"How did you get David's fingerprints for comparison?" I wanted to know.

128

"Police in Sydney went around to his home and took fingerprints from there. We have also been looking at CCTV around the Blackdown National Park for the week following 30 July, when David last rang his wife. We found a 2007 HiLux being driven by a man who closely resembles David. It's grainy, but we do believe it's him. Unfortunately, the passenger was looking down when the photo was taken and we couldn't see if there was anyone else in the back seats. The vehicle is registered to an address which turns out to be a vacant block of land. We're pretty sure the name on the registration, Greg Mainsbridge, is false too. Our database doesn't show anything under that name and we're pretty sure that whoever killed Jayden would have form."

"What colour is this HiLux?"

"It's black. We've circulated the details and the number plate so we're hopeful we will soon have some news for you."

"You have been busy, detective. Can you tell us the number plate?"

"No, that's confidential at this stage. We want this killer caught as much as you do. It's not good for Rockhampton's image to have a killer running around in the area."

"No, I don't suppose it is," Emma agreed.

After the call, Emma contacted the funeral parlour and let them know that Jayden's body would be released tomorrow morning. They promised to arrange collection as soon as possible and the funeral was arranged for Friday afternoon. I rang Mike, so that he could arrange his work commitments to attend and then I rang Sandra, so that she could arrange for someone to pick up Avril and Bethany from school on Friday.

That night, I continued our bedtime stories with the time Sandra and I went on a cruise from Sydney to London. A couple of nights into our cruise, a young woman fell overboard in the night. Had she fallen, was she pushed or had she committed suicide? It was on this same cruise that I met Mike and Sandra first met David.

It was mid-morning before we began the long drive back to Sydney. Emma wanted to drive first.

"I don't know how I can possibly help to find David, or to find Jayden's killer," I confessed. "I don't even know where to start. I only know that I can't sit around at home whilst David is somewhere in Queensland and Sandra is going frantic."

"Me too," Emma commented.

"What I am fervently hoping is that the police will find him, and Jayden's murderer, whilst we are in Sydney."

"Amen to that!"

We stopped overnight at the same caravan park at Coolangatta where we had stayed on the journey up. I rang Mike and Sandra whilst Emma made a couple of call to friends to let them know about the funeral. We bought fish and chips and sat at a table in the caravan park to eat them. Then I went around the groups of people sitting outside their caravans and showed them David's photo. It was worth one last effort, I thought, but no-one remembered seeing him or the camper.

On the drive back to Sydney a thought occurred to me.

"Emma, you don't believe that David killed Jayden, do you?"

Emma was quiet for a moment. "No, not really. I mean, I don't know what happened, but I can't imagine any reason why David would want to kill him and become a fugitive. He wouldn't be able to go home to his wife and children, so why would he do it? Besides, as you pointed out to the police, he would have needed a vehicle to get away, so why wouldn't he have taken Jayden's? No, that doesn't make any sense to me."

I sighed with relief. I would have hated to think that Emma was harbouring thoughts that David might have been responsible.

Changing the subject, I asked about her hobby farm at Windsor, situated not far out of Sydney. She had told me a little about it and I knew that they had an old horse that someone had retired on to their property, a cow which had been a family pet until the family who owned it returned to live in the suburbs, two kelpie dogs and an old cat, plus some chickens. Her neighbour had been keeping an eye on them whilst we had been away.

"I expect old Jack will be happy to keep an eye on them a bit longer," she replied. "He only has a small house block now and misses the land he had when he was younger. He enjoys pottering around the animals. I might have to cook him a few meals whilst I'm home though!"

I saw the glimmer of a smile and was glad she had someone to go home and talk to.

The traffic was heavy as we approached Sydney and it took as an hour longer than we had anticipated, but at last Emma pulled up in front of my apartment at Gladesville.

"Would you like to come in for a cup of tea?" I asked, knowing that she was going home to an empty house.

"No thanks, Anna. I think I'll head on home. Got to do it sometime," she replied, gruffly.

"Ring me anytime you like. You know, if you want to talk," I said, as I took my bags out of the campervan.

She nodded and I could see tears in her eyes. I gave her a long hug, then she climbed back into the vehicle and I watched her drive away.

Mike was still at work, so I unpacked, had a cup of coffee and enjoyed the luxury of space after the cramped conditions of the campervan. The thought of sharing my bed with Mike tonight made me smile.

When Mike came through the door, he swooped me up in his arms and twirled me around.

"It's so good to have you back," he said, kissing me enthusiastically.

"I can't tell you how good it is to be back!"

I sat on the sofa and he poured us both a glass of white wine.

"I'm sure you only missed my cooking," I joked.

"That too, I must confess. Speaking of which, would you like to go out for dinner tonight or are you cooking?"

"Dinner's all prepared. It will be lovely to eat at home, but thanks for the offer."

Before we ate, I rang Sandra and arranged to go over and see her in the morning. She was tearful and upset and I knew it had been a very difficult time for her.

Mike and I talked until late in the evening and, when we finally went to bed, it felt so good to snuggle into the body I had missed so much.

When I arrived at Sandra's the next day, she literally fell into my arms. I hugged her close and when she finally broke away, I could see the strain that the last few weeks had placed on her. She looked ten years older, her face lined, her eyes red and puffy and her hair unkempt.

"Oh, Sandra. I don't know what to say."

"It's great to see you, Anna. I can't wait to talk to you. You have to tell me everything."

Sandra's father and mother were sitting in the lounge and greeted me warmly. They had always been very kind and generous to me and I felt for them. They too looked very tired. I knew they were well into their eighties now and coping with Sandra's grief, as well as helping to look after the girls, would have been tough for them. Her father, Colin, was a tall, thin man, but he seemed to have developed a slight stoop in the years since I had seen him. Her mother, Irene, looked tired and drawn. Sandra's brother, Richard, emerged from the kitchen, grabbing me around my waist. He turned me around and kissed me on the cheek.

"Hi Anna. How are you?" he asked as he hugged me warmly and planted a kiss on my other cheek. I knew that he lived on the Central Coast now, with his wife and three sons. He was two years older than Sandra and had the same penetrating, green eyes and red hair.

"Richard, how lovely. I didn't expect to see you here," I replied.

"Well, I wanted to be here when you spoke to Sandra and my parents. We all want to know anything you can tell us."

"I wish I had more news," I replied, feeling totally inadequate. I could feel the expectation in the room and my heart sank, knowing that I had nothing to offer them that would be helpful or ease their pain.

Sandra's mother made coffee and placed some biscuits on the coffee table between us. I spent the next hour or so telling them about our trip and how Jayden's body was discovered. I told them how Emma and I had gone to the Blackdown Tableland National Park as she wanted to see where Jayden was found. He had already been taken to Rockhampton by ambulance by the time we arrived but the police were still there and they had a couple of sniffer dogs. They couldn't find any scent of David away from the crime scene, so they were pretty certain that he wasn't in the area. I tentatively mentioned that one of the theories the police had was that David could have shot Jayden, but the police had already run this past Sandra, so she wasn't shocked. I told them that I had pointed out that neither of the men had a gun, that David would never shoot anyone and that he would have needed to take Jayden's vehicle to get away and therefore this avenue of investigation seemed to have been discounted. When I had finished, they all had questions, but I was unable to shed any light as to what had happened or where David was now.

I stayed until lunchtime. Before I left, I retrieved a bag of David's clothes from my car, along with his personal items; toothbrush, comb, shampoo and toothpaste, which the police had released. Sandra took the bag from me, a small sob escaping as she did so. I kissed her goodbye and told her that Mike and I would pick her up tomorrow, half-an-hour before Jayden's funeral.

Chapter Twelve
The Day of the Funeral

The next morning it was raining heavily. *Fitting for a funeral*, I thought. I was glad that it was going to be a cremation and we wouldn't have to stand at a graveside in the rain. It would be difficult enough for all of us as it was.

Mike drove us to Sandra's and she came out in a pair of black trousers and a dark blue jumper, over which she wore a black jacket. I too wore black trousers, but had teamed mine with a dark grey jacket and light grey jumper. We waved to her parents, who were standing at the front door. I sat in the back with Sandra and held her hand. She had made her eyes up heavily to disguise the effects of the ever-present tears. I wondered how she was going to get through the funeral. I am sure she would be wondering if she would soon be going to a funeral for her own husband.

Emma was already at the crematorium when we arrived, standing at the door to greet people. Next to her was a woman in her twenties, who was obviously her daughter, Angie. She had her mother's hooded eyes and stocky build. I took her hand and said how sorry I was to meet her under these circumstances, then moved to Emma and held her tight for a moment. She looked exhausted and I could only imagine what it had been like for her to go back to their hobby farm on her own. Sandra and Emma embraced for a long while and both had tears in their eyes when they broke apart. We took our seats and the service began not long afterwards. We learned that Jayden had grown up on a farm, loved country life and camping and that he was Emma's soulmate. There were sounds of sniffling and sobbing throughout the service for a friend taken from them way too soon and in such horrific circumstances. After the coffin disappeared behind the curtain, we adjourned to a small reception room, where we drank coffee we didn't want and nibbled on small slices of cake. There were probably fifty people there and I could hear people whispering about Jayden's death and theories as to what had happened to him. I had the opportunity to speak with Angie briefly and she told me she was going to stay with her mother for a couple of days. Emma introduced me to their friend, Sam, who had lent us his campervan. Like everyone else, he was in a state of shock over Jayden's death. I thanked him for the loan of his campervan and left him to talk to his friends.

Mike dropped us off at Gladesville so that I could drive Sandra home whilst he went on to work. We had more coffee at the apartment first and talked about what could have happened to David. Sandra seemed almost resigned to the fact that he was dead; lying in the bush being eaten by wild animals. I tried to convince her that there was a good chance he was still alive, since his body hadn't been found near Jayden's.

"I think the killer, or killers, must have taken David with him – or them. It's the only thing that makes any sense. I'm sure David will do everything possible to stay alive and wait for an opportunity to escape. Then he will have to make it to a road or a house or something and the first thing he will do is ring you. Please, Sandra, you have to believe that he is still alive, if only for the girls. Don't give up on him yet. I know it's been over three weeks since he was due home...."

"Three weeks and a day."

"He could be way out in the bush somewhere, injured, with no mobile phone reception. We know he doesn't have his mobile phone anyway, because it was found in Jayden's vehicle. That doesn't mean he's dead. You have to believe he is coming back to you."

I made us both a sandwich. She ate half of it, which

139

was better than nothing. When I drove her home, her mother made more coffee and I stayed for a while longer.

"When are you going back to look for David?" Sandra asked as I was getting into the car.

"As soon as Emma is ready and the police release the slide-on camper. Probably not long after her daughter goes home on Sunday afternoon. I think she'll want something to do. You have to realise though, Sandra, that I don't know where to look. We can drive around the area and ask people if they have seen David, but it will be sheer luck if I can find him. We have to hope that David turns up somewhere of his own accord."

"I know, Anna. I can't even suggest anything, but please, keep looking. I trust you to find him for me."

I drove away feeling her expectations on my shoulders and little in the way of hope that I could find David. There were hundreds of kilometres of bush out there and I only had the Blackdown Tableland National Park as a starting point.

I rang Emma the next day, to see how she was going. She sounded resolute in her need to do something to find Jayden's killer.

"I want to fly back to Rockhampton as soon as we can.

I can't stand being here without Jayden. Detective Brady rang late last night to say they will be releasing the camper Monday morning. They didn't find any clues there at all. There were some fingerprints on Jayden's wallet. They were mainly from one of the men who found him, the rest were obliterated."

"It's a pity they touched it. I can't imagine the killer having much interest in Jayden's vehicle, if he didn't take his wallet or phone. I can leave Monday, if we can book flights. Why don't you leave that to me? I'll ring you back. In the meantime, can you think about what we are going to do when we get back to Rockhampton? Where are we going to start looking?"

"I've been thinking about it ever since the funeral and I can't say I know the answer. I'm still hoping that the police will have some sort of lead by the time we get to Rockhampton."

"So am I."

I was able to book us on a flight early Monday morning. I knew Mike would not be happy and he wasn't.

"You will be driving around aimlessly, with no idea where to look. David's body could be anywhere – you could be standing close by and not know it was there. Apart from that, there is a killer out there somewhere and, if he finds out that you are trying to track him down, he might decide to kill you too. Didn't your close encounter in France teach you anything?"

"I know what you are saying, darling and, yes, it did. I don't want to meet up with Jayden's killer, I only want to find David. I don't know where to start and I don't know where to look, but I'm hoping the police will find him before we get back to Rockhampton and then we can turn around and drive back home. In the meantime, Sandra has begged me to keep looking – what else can I do?"

Seeing it was a losing argument, Mike stopped trying to persuade me not to go and asked me how I would like to spend our Sunday together.

"A long lie-in, in our comfortable bed, would be a good start, considering I'll be back sharing a bed with Emma soon. Then maybe a drive and lunch out somewhere?"

"Done!"

"We should probably call in on Sandra on the way home."

"If we must."

"You'll enjoy seeing the girls."

"That's true."

"I'd better start packing."

We stayed in bed until after nine and had a light breakfast, before driving to my favourite beach, Balmoral. We had a long walk along the water's edge and enjoyed lunch at a restaurant overlooking the bay. It was perfect. Balmoral has beautiful, soft sand, a protected bay for swimming and a little island, joined by a small bridge, in the middle. With huge, Moreton Bay Fig trees on the grass behind the promenade, it was ideal for picnicking families and, on a Sunday, it was always packed. Some brave people were swimming, even in September. Later that afternoon, we drove go Glenhaven to see Sandra and the girls. Mike played ball with them, in the garden and Sandra's father joined in. Sandra, her mother and I stayed in the lounge talking. There was still no news of David and Sandra was becoming more despondent. Her mother told me, when she was out of the room, that she had even been talking about a memorial service.

"Surely not! It's way too soon. I can't believe David isn't alive. You have to talk her out of it."

"I'll do my best, but you know what she's like. Anyway, she won't do anything until you come back from Queensland."

Chapter Thirteen
Back on the Road

Emma caught the train to the airport and so did I, as Mike had to work. We met at the check-in queue and I was shocked at the change in Emma in only a couple of days. Her face was drawn and pale, her eyes puffy and she had lost weight since we set off last time. *Grief is ageing*, I thought.

Once we were on the plane, I asked her how her mother was.

"Had she missed you?"

"I think so. She seemed to be aware that I hadn't been for a while."

"It must be hard. I know you would have wanted her sympathy."

"I told her that Jayden had died. She seemed to know who Jayden was and said she was sorry to hear that, but I'm not sure that she understood. There wasn't any warmth or compassion in her voice. She didn't ask how he had died and I didn't tell her."

"Probably for the best."

"As I was leaving, she asked me to send her regards to Jayden."

"Her memory is that bad?"

"Yes, it is. Sometimes she can remember things that happened years ago, but most of the time she repeats the same things, asks the same questions."

Orphaned at the age of four, I had no real memories of my mother or father. It was my mother's older, unmarried sister, Aunt Jesse, who had brought me up. It was a huge loss to me when she died at the age of fifty-two, when I was barely eighteen. I had missed her dreadfully in those early years, but at least I hadn't watched her mind slowly fading away.

We caught a taxi from Rockhampton airport to the police station to reclaim the slide-on camper.

"Good afternoon, Mrs Watson, Mrs Davies," Detective John Brady said, shaking hands, "You're here to take the vehicle home, are you?"

"Not exactly, Detective," I responded. "We're here to try to find David Pearson."

"And my husband's killer," Emma added.

"Ah, well, that's probably not very wise, ladies. Not with a killer running around out there somewhere."

"Well, we're here to help you find him," Emma informed him, resolutely.

I could feel the conversation becoming tense.

"Look, Detective, I've promised Mrs Pearson that I'll try to find her husband. I know it's almost impossible; we don't even know where to start looking. Naturally, Mrs Watson wants to see her husband's killer brought to justice. Is there anything you have found out, which might help us? We're happy to leave you to search for the killer, we are here to try to find Mr Pearson."

Emma started to say something and I gave her a swift kick, which I hoped Detective Brady didn't notice.

"So far, I have to say, we haven't advanced much. We've had the results back from the blood found on the wheel brace and it didn't belong to Jayden or David. That leads us to believe it belongs to the killer but nothing came up on our database. There were fingerprints on the wheel brace from both Jayden and David, but not from anyone else. Like you, we have no idea where David Pearson is; we can only hope that someone comes across him. Or," he added quickly, seeing my expression, "that he turns up somewhere."

"I see."

"We've searched Blackdown Tableland National Park with the dogs and found nothing. If he went with the killer, to be honest, he could be anywhere by now. It could be that the killer was injured somehow and he took

Mr Pearson with him to do the driving. It would appear that the blood found at the scene might belong to him."

"That makes sense, I suppose."

"At least we haven't heard of any other murders in the area, so it doesn't look like there's a serial killer on the loose. Queensland is a huge State and we can't be sure that they are still in Queensland."

I inhaled swiftly. I didn't want to think about a serial killer or that David could be in another State by now.

"I suppose you have looked at murders in other States too?" I asked.

"Not really."

"Then how do you know there isn't a serial killer on the loose?"

The detective stroked his chin and stared at me.

"Maybe that is something we should look into. Anyway," he said, jumping up quickly, "I won't hold you two ladies up. I'll be in touch if we find anything new, or if Mr Pearson turns up. Good luck in your search and please, be careful. I don't want anything to happen to you. In fact, I'd be much happier if you would go home and leave it to us."

We thanked the detective for his concern and promised to be careful. We intimated that we would probably head for home in a couple of days, by a circuitous route.

We stopped the camper at a park to do some housekeeping. I found Jayden's bag and quietly added to it any of his clothes and personal items. Emma collected a few opened jars and threw them in the bin at the park. Then she sat down and made a list of what we would need to buy. Our next stop was at a supermarket to restock. Once that was done, I made some sandwiches and we returned to the park to eat them.

"Where to first? Any ideas?" I asked Emma as I ate the last of my sandwich.

She shrugged and I could tell that her heart wasn't in this. All the energy seemed to have drained from her.

"I think we should assume David is, or was, with the killer. Actually, he probably isn't with him anymore. I don't believe David wouldn't have seized an opportunity to get away from him, by now. Logically, the fact that he hasn't turned up anywhere means he must either be so far out in the bush and walking or he is holed up somewhere, injured. It's starting to heat up here now during the day, but the nights are still cool, so if he can find enough water, he could be walking at night."

"He won't be walking at night!" Emma scoffed. "You

can't walk in the bush at night when you don't know where you are going."

"Okay, well, he's been missing a long while, so I don't actually believe he is walking. I'm thinking more that he's been injured. What do you think about that?

"Sounds plausible. If you want my honest opinion though, I think he's dead too. In which case, it would make more sense to go looking for the killer."

I said nothing for a while. Emma pulled out a map and spread it across the table.

"Might as well stick a pin in it," she said, after looking at it for a few minutes.

"We need to be more rational than that. Look, when they left the National Park, which direction do you think the killer would have taken?"

"Inland. If they were looking to hide, they wouldn't have gone towards the coast."

"Exactly. So do you think they would have headed towards Longreach, or down Charleville way?"

"More likely Charleville way," she said, after some thought.

"Well, how about we head out to Barcaldine and then down to Charleville."

"I'm thinking, rather than going back to Emerald and

Barcaldine, we should go via the Great Inland Way, south from Emerald, down to Roma and then across to Charleville."

"Good as anything. That's a plan then. Let's go!"

Chapter Fourteen
A New Hobby

I took the wheel and we headed for Springsure. The slide-on camper was heavier to drive than the campervan, but I soon adjusted to it. The drive south from Emerald was pretty uninspiring. Lots of dry bush, each kilometre looking much the same as the last. Mike had a point, I thought. The scenery in England was so pretty, with lots of lush, green grass, tall trees which often formed a tunnel across the road, fields full of crops. There was still the matter of the weather, though. Grey skies and rainy days. Cold, gusty winds. Here the sun was beating down, the sweat running down my back underneath my cotton shirt. Thank goodness for the vehicle's air-conditioning. As the sparse trees and bush whizzed past us, I knew that David could be lying out there somewhere and we would never see him. What had made me think I had any chance of finding him?

We arrived at Springsure mid-afternoon and booked into a caravan park. Emma had been quiet all day. It seemed to me she was very depressed and I didn't know what to say or do to make things better. Once we booked in, Emma took the wheel and expertly parked our camper near the ablutions block. Then she showed me how everything worked. It was clever the way a sink pulled out from the side, the roof raised to reveal a bed in the middle of a small room and a camping stove. Clever, but very compact. This was to be my new home for goodness knows how long, I thought with a sigh. At Happy Hour that evening, we mingled with the other campers, showing them the photo of David. We explained that he could be wandering around, disorientated, or maybe lying dead in the bush somewhere. We also told them about Jayden and warned them that there was a killer running around loose somewhere, which didn't go down too well. Some of the wives looked apprehensive and I heard a couple of them begging their husbands to stick to the more popular routes and not to consider off-road camping.

One of the entrances to the Carnarvon National Park was at Springsure. Nearly three hundred thousand acres of park, I discovered when I googled it on my phone. Was it worth having a look in the park? If you were hiding, would you go into a National Park? It was a huge area, but a lot of campers went to National Parks, so our killer might go somewhere more secluded. We didn't even know who the killer was, let alone how he thought.

I asked Emma whether she considered it was worth looking there.

"I don't know, Anna. He might have gone in there for water. It's hard to say."

"This is hopeless!" I declared. "We are never going to find either of them. It's absolutely impossible."

"Oh, well. At least we are heading towards home. You can tell Sandra you tried."

At the mention of Sandra, I tensed. My best friend, how could I not try to help? I thought of Avril and Bethany, their innocent faces appearing in front of me. I couldn't bear to see them streaked with tears because their father wasn't coming home.

"I had been hoping that the police would have come up with something; some kind of clue, to set us in the right direction."

"So had I, but they don't seem to have any more idea than we do."

"So true."

"How about another one of your bedtime stories?"

We went to bed, the dilemma of the National Park unresolved. This time I told Emma about my missing author in London, who disappeared, along with his manuscript, when I was working as a Senior Editor.

After a good night's sleep, my determination to find David had returned. We decided to spend the morning in Springsure, showing David's photo to people. Emma took one side of the main street and I took the other. I spoke to many of the shop-keepers as well as shoppers. Whilst in Sydney I had arranged to have another five hundred posters printed and it was not hard to persuade the shop-keepers to let me put a copy in their window. About half-way down the street, a man ran up behind me and tapped me on the shoulder.

"Excuse me," he said, "but I think I saw the man you are looking for."

I turned to face him. He was an older man, probably in his sixties, with long, grey hair and bushy eyebrows. His red, pocked nose led me to believe that he might enjoy a drink or two in the evenings. He had one of my posters in his hand and he pointed at David's photo.

"This man you're looking for, I think I saw him."

"Did you? Where did you see him?"

"He was in the pub at the end of the street," he replied, pointing further up the road."

"When was this?"

"Two nights ago. I'm sure it was the same man."

My heart was pounding, at the thought that I could be

155

so close to David.

"What time did you see him?"

"It was about ten o'clock, not long before I left. He was sitting on a bar stool on his own, enjoying a beer."

"Thank you so much, Mr.....?"

"Jameson. You're welcome. I hope you find him soon."

I walked up the street, opposite to where Emma was talking to a young woman, and beckoned for her to come across. As soon as she had finished talking, she crossed the road.

"We may have a lead on David. A man thinks he saw him in the pub up there," I said, pointing up the hill, "two nights ago."

"Let's go then."

The pub had only been open a few minutes and the man behind the bar looked up as we walked in.

"Hello. We are looking for this man," I said, holding up David's photo, "and a man in the street told me he thought he was in here two nights ago."

The bartender took a good look at the photo and shook his head.

"I haven't seen him, I'm afraid. I was working that

night, but I don't recognise him. What time was it?"

"About ten. He said he was sitting at a bar stool, drinking by himself."

"There was someone drinking alone, but he didn't look like him. Who told you he saw him?"

"A Mr Jameson."

"Ah, well, you don't want to take too much notice of Alf Jameson. He means well, but he can't see two foot in front of his nose. No, I'm sorry, I'm sure your man wasn't in here."

I was so disappointed. I had thought we had a clue at last.

"Would you mind putting up one of our posters?" Emma asked.

"Not at all, love. Leave one with me."

We left the pub and went back to talking to people on the street. I felt totally deflated and it was becoming hard to find much enthusiasm. When I reached the top of the street, I turned to see how far behind me Emma was. As I did, I noticed a man getting out of a black Toyota HiLux 4WD a few yards away. I thought how ill he looked. He was only late twenties, early thirties maybe. He was gaunt and pale and it occurred to me he was probably a junkie. He looked around, furtively I thought, before taking out a cigarette and lighting it, whilst leaning against the car door. For some reason, I pulled out my phone and took a photo of him. As he walked down the street, I moved so that I could take a photo of his number plate. I decided I was going to take photos of any suspicious-looking men with a black Toyota HiLux everywhere we went, even if I didn't know if it was a 2007 model. Photography would be my new hobby. Who knows, maybe I might capture our killer! It would have been helpful if the police had given me the number plate of the suspected vehicle. Then I would have known if I was photographing the right one!

"What are you doing?" Emma asked, as she joined me.

I told her of my plan and she laughed.

"Whatever makes you feel useful," she said.

By mutual agreement, we decided not to tackle the Carnarvon National Park. It seemed like a daunting task, so we continued on to Rolleston instead. In a valley with rich black soil, the area produces great vegetables. We would have lunch in one pub and a drink in another and talk to some of the people. As it turned out, there was only one pub, so it wasn't too taxing. We had a reasonable chicken parmigiana and a couple of beers before we started again. Whilst people were happy to talk to us, no-one remembered seeing David.

We left Rolleston for the short drive to Injune, which was quite pretty. I was still doing the driving, Emma not showing any interest in doing so, but we were not going very far each day, so it didn't worry me. This 4WD was nicer to drive than the campervan, I decided, now that I had become used to it.

I photographed two possible subjects in Injune. The first was a man in his forties, with a scruffy, black beard which covered half of his face. He was standing by a HiLux which was covered in dust and dirt but I could still see that it was black in colour. It looked as if it hadn't been washed for months and he looked as if he had been living wild in the bush himself. I couldn't tell how old the Toyota was, but I photographed it anyway. The next time I saw a Toyota HiLux, it was parked in the main street of Injune. Once again it was covered in dust and dirt, but it didn't look very old to me. I took a snap of the number plate anyway and then waited for the owner to come back and claim it. Fortunately, I only had to wait about twenty minutes before a man, who looked to be in his twenties from where I was standing, headed towards it. I snapped him as he opened the door.

Injune was an interesting town, with an old courthouse, a coal mine, art gallery and cemetery. Once again, I wished I could do some sightseeing, but I reminded myself that wasn't why we were here. It attracted quite a few tourists, so it was a good opportunity to talk to people who had travelled around the area. Maybe here we would find someone who had seen David. Once again, it provided access to the Carnarvon National Park – what a huge area that park covers!

We put up posters, talked to all sorts of locals and travellers, but the answer was always the same. No-one had seen anyone who resembled David.

"For all we know, David and the killer might not even be in Queensland," I moaned to Emma later in the day. "They could be in New South Wales by now."

"Or the Northern Territory, for that matter. We always knew it was a long shot. I think we both wanted to take some action, rather than sitting around at home."

"Well, the next town is Roma and then we have to decide whether we keep going south to Sydney, or go east along the Warrego Highway towards Quilpie."

Emma's sad eyes looked into mine. "I'm not ready to go home, yet," she whispered.

"Besides," she said a little while later. "We haven't done any off-road camping yet. We've been in a caravan park every night. That's not real camping!"

The thought of 'real camping' didn't excite me very much, but I think Emma already knew that!

Chapter Fifteen
Free Camping

Our next stop was Mitchell, where there is an open-air spa. Whilst neither Emma nor I wished to sample the spa, (we hadn't packed our swimsuits, anyway), we did think it would be a good place to catch up with a number of travellers. I had imagined the spa to be in a natural setting, surrounded by rocks and grass, not the formal swimming pool we encountered. Despite my initial disappointment, it was very pleasant and we spent most of the day there, talking to people from all around Australia. None of them had seen David. I took one photo of a Toyota HiLux (I could pick one out easily, by now) with its wild-looking driver, whose grey hair was pulled back into a long pony-tail.

Late in the afternoon, Emma took the wheel and we went back on the road to look for a suitable place to free-camp. About three-quarters of an hour later, she pulled off the highway down a narrow road, and a couple of kilometres along, she found a place to pull in. It was a stony, dusty area encircled by gum trees.

"There's not enough room for anyone else to pull in here, so we should be safe enough," she offered.

We set up the camper and Emma began to prepare dinner. She seemed to have snapped out of her depression and was all business. I was glad to have her bustling around again. It was dark by the time we had washed the plates and pan in the small amount of water she dished out from our reserves. I was not impressed at washing myself in an equally small bowl of water, nor at having to venture into the bush, torch in hand, to relieve myself before settling down for the night. I could hear rustling in the bushes and a magpie saying goodnight and I hurried back to the trailer as fast as I could, resolving not to make another trip before dawn.

"Tonight, I'll tell you my last story, which happened quite recently, when Mike and I were in France for two years. In fact, we had only been back in London for four months afterwards when this contract in Sydney came up."

Emma listened intently whilst I told her about the children who had disappeared in France over several years. When I had finished my story, she let out a sigh. "You have had some interesting times. It's hard to believe all that happened to one person."

"Well, it has been over a number of years. Most of it was a case of being in the right place at the right time to make the connections.

"And now, this mystery. I only hope we can achieve as good a result."

"Well, it won't be for lack of trying."

"That's for sure!"

"Anyway, I've promised Mike I won't get involved again, once David is found."

Emma gave me a look that said she clearly didn't believe me, but this was one promise I had every intention of keeping.

I woke repeatedly during the night, thinking I had heard someone outside the trailer. I lay awake in the dark, listening to the unaccustomed noises of the bush, straining for any indication that the killer was about to fling open the door and kill us in our bed.

The next morning, when Emma handed me a small shovel to take into the bush to dig a hole for my daily ritual, I knew for certain that I was never going to take to camping. However, when I stepped behind the trailer, I saw a mob of about thirty grey kangaroos in a clearing across the road. I watched them for a while and saw a baby stick its head out of mum's pouch, before extricating himself (or maybe, herself?) and hopping along beside mum for a while. He, or she, nibbled on something, before hopping back inside the pouch. To see them close up and so unafraid of humans, I had to admit, was something pretty special.

After another unsatisfactory wash, a cup of coffee and some cereal, Emma manoeuvred the vehicle out of our camping spot, turned it around and put us back on the road. I knew I had been lucky that it made more sense up until now to stay in a caravan park, where we could talk to people and show them David's photograph, than to free-camp. I suspected Emma's preference would always be free-camping!

We stopped to speak to people in Mungallala, again without any success, before moving on to the tiny town of Morvan. By now, red dust was permeating everything inside the vehicle and the camper. I could taste it at the back of my throat and feel it in my hair. The wind blew it across the bed, the sink and every other surface. At first, I had tried to wipe it off, but it came back before I had even finished cleaning. In the end I took Emma's advice and tried to ignore it, but it was in my clothes when I shook them out and even on my toothbrush! I was glad that, because we were going from town to town, we had kept to the sealed roads and not gravel ones.

I found another HiLux to photograph in Morvan. Covered in red dust, the number plate was nearly obscured, but I was able to stand close enough to it that it was readable. I looked around for the owner and he soon appeared out of the bakery, with a pie and can of coke in his hand. He was in his forties, I judged, with long dark brown hair and a sunburnt face. I stood back under a shop awning and zoomed in on his face. I managed to snap him without him noticing.

I hadn't been able to speak to Mike or Sandra last night, as there was no phone reception so I made for the Morven Museum where, I had discovered earlier from Google, there was a handcrafted miniature building display which had taken over fifteen years to complete. I was amazed that a town of only approximately two hundred and fifty people would have its own museum, but understood when I found the little slab hut in which it was housed. Nearby was the tin hut built from flattened kerosene tins. Having had a quick look at the display of the pioneer village, I used their phone reception to ring Mike.

"I hate this free-camping!" I exclaimed when he answered.

"I knew you would! How's it going otherwise?"

"Oh, the same old, same old. We talk to people and show them David's photo but no-one recognises him. Sandra hasn't heard anything, I suppose?"

"No, I spoke to her last night. I'm starting to worry about her, Anna. She isn't coping very well. Thank goodness her parents are there with her."

"Yes, that's something at least. Well, I won't hold you up at work. I wanted to let you know we are okay. Haven't bumped into that killer yet!"

"Make sure you don't. Take care, speak to you soon."

Next, I rang Sandra.

"No news, I'm afraid. We're about halfway between Roma and Charleville. I had my first night of free-camping last night and I'm not a fan."

"Thank you, Anna. I know you are only doing this for me and it can't be much fun. It's hard to imagine you camping!"

"I'm sure we'll have a good laugh about it later."

"You haven't found anyone who has seen David?"

"Only an old man who thought he saw him at the local pub, but the bartender said David was never there and not to take any notice of his alcoholic customer."

"The police have had calls from all over Australia, but

nothing has checked out yet. One person claimed to have seen Jayden and David two days after Jayden had been killed! It's great that people take the time to contact the police, but most of the calls are false leads."

"It must be so frustrating for the police, who have to check them out."

"I'm still hoping that one of them will lead to David."

"Me too. I've been taking photos of every suspicious looking man I've come across with a HiLux. I'm going to send them to Detective Brady, maybe it will lead to something. I'll ring you again soon. Maybe one of us will have some news then. Hang in there, Sandra."

Next, I sent the photos I had taken to Detective Brady, asking him to check out the vehicles and drivers. It didn't take long to elicit a phone call from the detective.

"You know the chances of these drivers who, by the way, didn't have a passenger, being the murderer are less than zero," he informed me. I thought I detected a smile in his voice though. He said he would have them checked out anyway and let me know if anything came of them. He gave me the impression I shouldn't hold my breath.

It didn't take long to put up a few posters around the

small town and talk to the locals. Again, we drew a blank and soon we were back on the road, heading for Charleville. There were a lot of mulga trees towards Charleville.

"That's because they're good in drought," Emma had informed me, when I commented on them before. "They've got a long tap root so they can reach down a long way to find water."

We'd been driving for about an hour and I had my eyes closed, drifting, when Emma nudged my arm.

"Look over there, Anna!" she said, pointing to our right.

"Camels!" I exclaimed.

"Yep, lots of wild camels in Australia."

I looked in wonder at the herd of some forty, one-humped camels walking along beside us, not far from the road.

"There's a baby!" I squealed in delight. "And another!"

"They're not wild ones, actually. It's a camel farm. You can go there and pat them and buy camel milk and other camel products."

That was when I noticed the fence.

"Most of the wild camels are in the Northern

Territory or South Australia. There are some in Queensland, but not as many. They were released by their owners with the arrival of motorised transport and the lack of cameleers. With no predators, there are now about three hundred thousand wild camels in Australia."

A little further along we passed the gate, which had a large sign advertising camel rides and camel products. There were definitely some interesting things to see in the outback, I thought, as we continued on to Charleville.

I was quite excited to see Charleville – a well-known outback town with a population of a little over three thousand people. It was a good-sized town, very flat, with many of the roads being unsealed, nothing but red dirt. By now, our vehicle was covered with red dust and so were we. Charleville is built along the Warrego River, a well-known fishing and camping spot. Fingerlings are released each year to ensure there is plenty of good fishing, Emma told me, and she said it was lovely camping under the red river gums. She and Jayden had camped there on a couple of occasions. I had googled Charleville on my phone and I knew that it had been flooded in 1990. The Warrego River had risen and the flood waters reached over eight metres. The whole town had been evacuated and many people were rescued by locals and their boats. Thanks to their efforts, not one life was lost. This was the first time in Australia a "Mud Army" had arrived. Now they appear regularly after floods around Australia, just ordinary people turning up to sweep mud out of houses, pull out the ruined furniture and help the townspeople to get back on their feet.

I would have loved to have had time to see the night sky at the Cosmos Centre or to see the place where they were breeding bilbies, but we weren't there to play at tourists. I knew bilbies were endangered marsupials with rabbit-like ears, a long nose and a long tail with a white tip, but I had never seen one. I wondered if David and Jayden had found time to enjoy some of the experiences available here. We showed David's photo at several of the tourist areas, as well as some cafes and shops, but there were no positive identifications, only a couple of 'maybe's'.

"We're not making much progress," Emma said, as we sat outside the camper eating sandwiches.

"I think we're going well," I responded, referring to

our journey.

"I meant in trying to find David, or Jayden's killer. We seem to be driving around aimlessly, asking the same questions and getting nowhere."

'I know, but what else can we do?"

"I don't know. Everything seems pointless without Jayden." She let out a deep sigh. "I would like to find out who killed him though."

"I don't see how we can. We have no idea who it was, why they did it, or where they are now. They could be hundreds of kilometres away from here by now, in another State. Do you want to give up and go home?"

Emma thought about this for a minute or two. She took her eyes off her sandwich for a moment, to meet mine.

"Nah. I think we'll keep going for a while longer."

Part Two

Chapter Sixteen
Jayden

There was a loud bang – the rifle went off and David watched as Jayden fell backwards. He moved towards him, but the shooter yelled at him to stay still. He stopped and turned towards him, unable to comprehend what had happened.

"You shot him!" David exclaimed.

"Yeah and I'll shoot you too, if you don't do as I say."

"Why did you shoot him?"

"He was going for something."

"I have to check him, see if he's still alive."

"Okay then," he shrugged. "Have a look - but don't do anything silly."

David rushed to Jayden's side. He was lying flat on his back, his eyes staring, a neat bullet hole in his forehead. He felt for a pulse in his neck, but found none. He already knew that Jayden was dead, but he was buying himself time, sensing that his own life was now in danger. The man they knew as Gary wasn't going to leave a witness to this murder. He could see the wheel brace Jayden had reached for, lying on the ground, only a foot away from him. The long bar with the tyre lever at one end and socket at the other would make a good weapon. If he could grab hold of it, he might have some sort of chance. Gary had already stood the rifle up against the trailer. He seemed to be in a daze. David didn't believe Gary had meant to kill Jayden, it was more like an instinctive action. It had all happened so fast.

"It was an accident, mate," David said, in a placating voice. "I know you didn't mean to shoot him. He's dead though."

Gary bent down beside Jayden and he too felt for a pulse, probably hoping that Jayden was only unconscious. Jayden's staring eyes told him everything he needed to know and the lack of pulse confirmed it. He was definitely dead. David realised that this was his best chance to escape from this killer. He was either going to kill him or take him along and he didn't fancy either option. Whilst Gary was busy transferring the money he had taken from Jayden's wallet into his own, David seized the opportunity; stretching out slowly, he grabbed the wheel brace, swinging it up and over his head. He brought it down with all his force, but Gary was too quick for him. He sprung to his feet and jumped away and it only caught his right foot. Gary screamed with pain and doubled over. David brought the wheel brace down on his foot a second time. Making the most of the opportunity, David raised the wheel brace again. He knew he should strike Gary in the head but, somehow, he couldn't bring himself to do that. He smashed it down across Gary's knee instead, on the same leg. Gary yelled, then quickly reached across to pick up the rifle. He straightened up and brought the rifle up to his shoulder, pointing it at David.

"You don't want to do that, Gary. One murder, well, it was an accident. Shoot both of us and it's definitely murder."

Gary hesitated.

"Get in," he yelled, hopping around on his left leg. "The driver's side. You'll have to drive. Thanks to you, I won't be able to use my right foot."

David wished now that he had used the second strike to hit Gary over the head. He bent down and closed Jayden's eyes.

"Sorry mate," he muttered, as he straightened up, knowing he was leaving him exposed to the elements. "I hope someone finds you soon and tells Emma."

He walked slowly back to the car. He considered

making a dash for it, but where was he going to go? Still, better to be stuck in the bush for a few hours than dead. He saw Gary look down at his smashed knee and foot. He was only wearing thongs, so David could see that the end of the wheel brace had inflicted considerable damage. His foot looked a funny shape, already starting to swell on top and it was bleeding heavily. If he ran into the bush, Gary wasn't going to follow him with that injury. Using the rifle as a walking stick, Gary hobbled towards the passenger seat. This might be his only chance to get away. He hesitated for a moment too long.

"Get in!" Gary shouted, waving the rifle at him. David knew that Gary was a pretty good shot. Should he chance it? He hung back, waiting for Gary to get inside, to give himself a head-start, but Gary stood there, leaning on the open door, pointing the rifle straight at him. He must have sensed his reluctance.

David sighed and moved to the driver's door. He got in, started the vehicle, put it in gear and drove away from his dead friend.

"Which way?" David asked, as they came out of the National Park.

"North, head north."

David turned right on to the Great Inland Way.

Gary kept one hand on the rifle between his legs whilst they drove. He had pulled out a grubby-looking rag and wrapped it around his injured foot. After a while, he pulled out the bag of gems he had stolen from them and emptied them into his hand.

"Not much of a stash. This one might be worth something," he commented, picking out the sapphire David had found on their second day of fossicking. Gary ran his forefinger over them, looking at them intently, before putting them back in the bag and stashing them in his shirt pocket.

David kept his eyes on the road ahead, whilst images of his wife and children flashed through his mind. He wondered if he would ever see them again. What were the chances of him getting out of this alive? Perhaps if Gary fell asleep? He didn't look as if he was going to fall asleep though. Still, he'd have to sleep some time. He relived again the moment when Gary had shot Jayden. He hadn't seen Gary fire the shot, he had been watching Jayden. One minute he was standing, the next he was falling backwards. David felt as if he was in shock, he had never seen anyone killed in front of him before.

Jayden hadn't deserved that. He'd been a good travelling companion, patient and happy to explain to David, a complete camping novice, what they were doing and why. Now Emma was a widow and she didn't even know it. How long would it be before someone found Jayden? Once they did, they would know he was missing. He hoped it wouldn't be too long.

After a couple of hours, Gary ordered him to take a dirt road off to the left. David's heart was thumping. Is this where his life was going to end?

"I need to have a look at this foot – see what damage you've done to it. Hurts like hell. Pull over there," Gary said, pointing to a clearing off the track.

"You stay here. Don't move. There's nowhere for you to hide and I won't hesitate to shoot."

Gary opened the door and eased himself outside, taking the rifle with him. At the back of the vehicle, he put his injured foot on the bumper bar and unwound the rag, which was soaked with blood.

"Holy hell! You've made a right mess of my foot!" he exclaimed. David watched him in the side mirror, as he shuffled things around in the back, pulling out a first aid kit.

"If you sit in the car I'll have a look at it for you, if you like," David offered.

Gary hopped back to the passenger seat and sat with his legs hanging out the door.

"Don't try anything!" Gary warned.

"I won't."

David rested Gary's foot on his knee. It was a mess. There was blood oozing from a nasty split over the knuckle of his big toe, which was flattened and obviously broken in at least one place. The toe next to the big one was sticking out at a funny angle, across the next toe. David didn't know what to do to try to fix it. He pulled out a wipe from the First Aid kit and cleaned off some of the blood, before sticking the largest plaster over the split. There was still blood coming from somewhere. David wiped the foot more thoroughly and could see a hole in the fleshy part between his big toe and the next one.

"Must have been something sharp on the end of that wheel brace. There's a hole between your toes."

"Well, put a bandaid over it."

"I think it needs more than a bandaid! You've got some broken toes here too. You need to see a doctor and have them set."

"I'm not going near any doctor. Can you splint them, or something?"

"Do you have any thing I can use as a splint?"

Gary thought for a while, his mind obviously running through the contents of the back of the vehicle.

"I don't think so," he said after a few minutes.

"You need to see a doctor."

"No doctor. Do the best you can."

David put some wadding and a plaster over the hole, but the foot was a mangled mess.

"I need to see if I can straighten the toe that's lying horizontal."

"Do it."

David had never tried to set a dislocated toe before and he didn't know how it was done. He knew you were supposed to yank it back into place. He took a tentative hold of it and pulled it out and then in the direction it should be facing and gave it a sharp tug. Gary screamed.

"That looks better, but I can't tell if it's in the right place."

"It'll do."

"Your third toe is broken too."

"Bandage them all together."

David used up the rest of the bandage, putting some

wadding underneath the foot to give it some padding. The result was a very large bandage that looked more like a football than a foot. David glanced at Gary's knee. It was swelling rapidly.

"Pass me the water bottle and a couple of those pain-killers from the bottom of the First Aid box," Gary ordered.

Gary gulped down the tablets and took a long drink of water. He held the water bottle out to David, who also drank thirstily.

"That's enough. We need to make it last until we can fill up again," Gary said, dusting his hat off by banging it on his knee.

"You still need to see a doctor. Your foot's not going to heal like that and I don't know what damage there is to your knee."

"Shut up and have a look in the back of the HiLux. There's a set of number plates in there somewhere. Dig them out and change them over."

Who carries a spare set of number plates around with them?" David wondered. He found the plates and a screwdriver and set about changing them over. When he had finished, Gary struggled to his feet and took the old plates from David. One-by-one he hurled them into the bush.

"Now, start driving. Turn this thing around and go back on the highway."

An hour later they were approaching the town of Clermont.

"Why don't we stop here and look for a doctor?" David asked.

"Don't want no doctor and we ain't stopping in this town, so keep driving."

David looked at him and wondered again what crimes Gary had committed previously. His dishevelled appearance indicated he had not had a shower or done any laundry for a while. He didn't smell too bad, but he was definitely in need of a good shower. His brown, straggly hair and beard were long and unkempt. When he had first seen him, David guessed him to be in his forties but now, seeing him close up, he figured late thirties. His brown eyes, which were narrow slits, were cold and uncaring. Shifty, is how David would have described them. They seemed to look straight through him, with no hint of compassion. Maybe he was a serial killer and that's why he didn't want to go near a doctor or town. Perhaps there was already a warrant out for him. David knew that he had to get away but it was going to be tricky. He would have to wait until Gary fell asleep.

A couple of hours later, Gary directed him to turn off the highway down another narrow dirt road. They drove for a couple of kilometres until Gary told him to pull in under some gum trees. He drove in and realised that the vehicle was barely visible from the track.

"I need to get some rest," Gary announced. He reached under his seat and pulled out a pair of handcuffs. What sort of person carries handcuffs, other than a policeman? Maybe he kept them for his sex life.

"Here, put your right hand on the steering wheel."

Knowing he had no choice, David complied. Gary made his way around to the driver's door, opening and quickly snapping the handcuff around David's wrist and the other one around the steering wheel. David was trapped. Then Gary opened his door and slipped into the dual cab behind. David had noticed earlier that it was littered with clothes, but Gary shifted them around and lay down on the back seat and promptly went to sleep. David had no choice but to sit patiently until he woke up a couple of hours later. Whilst he was waiting, he tried to think of a way out of this situation. If Gary was going to handcuff him to the steering wheel every time he went to sleep, not only was David not going to get much sleep but he had no chance of escaping. He had no idea how long Gary would keep him alive; probably until his foot healed sufficiently for him to drive himself. David thought it was more likely the foot would become infected or heal in such a way that Gary wouldn't be able to walk properly, if he didn't get proper medical attention. What was in his past that would stop him seeing a doctor?

By the time Gary awoke, David still didn't have a plan of escape. He would have to wait his chance and make sure he was ready to take advantage of the opportunity when it presented itself. Gary stretched and sat up.

"Time to eat something. You can cook. Got myself my own personal chef! There's a camping stove in the back and some tins of soup. There's also half a loaf of bread. Might be a bit stale, but it'll be alright soaked in the soup. You warm it up and, remember, I've got the rifle. There's a couple of chairs in the back too – put them out and I'll sit on one and watch you. You'll find some coffee there too. No tea, so hope you like coffee," he said with a sneer.

Gary limped around the front of the vehicle to the

driver's door and was careful undoing the handcuffs, so David had no chance to grab him with his free hand. He left the handcuffs attached to the steering wheel.

David pulled out the two fold-up chairs and set them out. It was unfortunate they were not the canvas-type, he thought, or Gary would have had great difficulty getting himself out of it and that might have bought him a few seconds. He found the camping stove and managed to light it. The soup tins had pull-rings so he emptied them into an old saucepan that had seen better days. There were a couple of tin dishes and plates and some cutlery in a box near the tailgate. David realised that he was starving and wondered what other food Gary was carrying. He could see another four tins of soup and a couple of cans of tinned meat, but that was all. Water would be their biggest problem, he knew. He had seen a large plastic bottle further inside, which he assumed was water.

"How are we off for water?" he asked.

"We're right for a bit."

David had to be satisfied with that. He didn't want to give Gary any reason to think he was a nuisance or a liability.

Whilst Gary slept stretched out on the back seat,

David tried to sleep sitting up, handcuffed to the steering wheel. It wasn't easy. He thought about Sandra and his girls. He knew how worried they would be when he and Jayden didn't arrive home around the promised date. Still, that was a couple of days away. Sandra wouldn't even know he was in trouble yet. Maybe he could escape before she even knew. How he wished he was home with them instead of out in the scrub with a dangerous lunatic! Why had he been so keen to do an outback trip? He hadn't even enjoyed it that much. Jayden was easy company and knowledgeable in the ways of the bush, but David hadn't liked sleeping in the swag outside the slide-on camper after the novelty wore off in the first couple of nights, or not having a hot shower. Most of the outback was pretty boring, he'd decided. Kilometre after kilometre of scrub or dry, dusty soil and, when you arrived at a town, it looked much the same as the last one. Jayden loved it though, he remembered. He seemed to enjoy every minute. He had told him how much he had missed going away with Emma recently, since her mum had become ill. He said the desert was different every time he travelled it and he never tired of it. David thought he should have holidayed with his family at the beach. Now he was in a fine mess. He nodded off a few times, only to wake with his head resting on the steering wheel and his handcuffed arm numb. How was he supposed to keep driving if he didn't get any sleep?

In the early hours of the morning Gary woke up and climbed back into the passenger seat, searching around for the First Aid kit. He found a couple more painkillers and took them with a swig of water.

"I'm going to unlock these handcuffs now. You climb in the back and get some sleep or you'll be no use to me. Don't think about trying anything funny, though. You know I'll shoot you if you do," Gary said, indicating the rifle he was still holding.

Grateful to be able to lie down and to have his arm free, David fell asleep almost immediately. Gary sat in one of the fold-up chairs, the rifle across his knees, watching him.

The next day, after a breakfast of tinned spam and the last of the dry bread, Gary ordered David to get back on the highway and keep driving north. When they arrived at Beylando Crossing, Gary told him to pull into the roadhouse and fill up with petrol. David looked around. There wasn't much here, except for the Roadhouse.

"Get some more painkillers, will yer? See what food they've got too. We need coffee, sugar and bread," Gary instructed, not moving from the passenger seat.

"What about meat?"

"There's meat where we're going, so that'll do. Be sure to get them pain killers, couple of packets. And pay cash, don't want anyone tracing your credit card. Don't go talking to no-one while you're doing it. If you try and get anyone to help you, I'll shoot you both."

David believed him. He wasn't going to risk anyone else's life. Gary didn't offer any money so he paid for the petrol and supplies with his own cash. When he returned to the vehicle, Gary told him to take the water container and fill it at the tap beside the roadhouse. A man was standing near the tap, having a cigarette. David kept his head down and pretended not to see him, whilst he filled the water container. As he moved away, the man nodded at him and David looked him straight in the eye, willing him to remember him.

About forty-five minutes down the road, Gary told David to take the next turning to the left. It was a dirt road and they followed it for about fifty kilometres, according to the speedometer, before Gary said to take the fork to the right. Where were they going? The narrow track went for another ten kilometres and eventually led to a small tin shed.

"This is it."

David took in his surroundings. There was nothing as far as the eye could see, only scrub and dirt, no sign of human habitation. It wasn't the sort of place anyone was going to drop in to say hello.

Gary used the rifle to hobble to the wooden door. It wasn't locked and when he gave it a shove, it opened inwards. The hut consisted of one room, with a single bed to one side, a table and a couple of chairs. Gary lowered himself on to one of the chairs and instructed David to bring the camping stove inside, along with the coffee, sugar and bread.

"Make me some coffee and give me a couple more of those painkillers."

There were mugs, plates and cutlery on a bench which ran along the length of the wall opposite the bed. Above it was a cupboard and the only window.

"There's food in there," Gary said, seeing David looking at the cupboard. "Have a look."

Inside the cupboard were tins of stew, meat and soup. At least they wouldn't starve. David was quite a good cook, having lived on his own for a while in his early twenties, but there were no spices here to improve the basic supplies available. At least there was a small bag of rice, he noted, which would make a change. He wondered how Gary knew the hut was here and whether this was where he had been living. How long were they going to be staying here?

"We'll share the bed. You can sleep during the day. Hey, there won't be much else to do anyways!" Gary informed him with a dry laugh.

Water was again going to be their problem, but when he mentioned it, Gary said there were four large containers of water under the bench. Pulling aside the dirty curtain underneath the bench, David found the water; a large, oval tin bowl, presumably for washing dishes; some soap and toilet paper.

David grabbed one of the containers of water and poured some into the kettle which he put on the camping stove to boil. He spooned coffee and sugar into two mugs and passed the packet of painkillers to Gary.

Six days passed in the hut. The days were hot now and the hut, being made of tin, was stifling; the days seemingly endless. David tried to make conversation with Gary, but he only grunted in reply. In the end, David gave up trying to talk to him. Gary kept the keys to the vehicle in his pocket at all times and the rifle never left his side. At night, when Gary slept, David was handcuffed to a small tree outside the hut. At least it was cooler at night. He soon became more relaxed with the sounds and rustlings of the bush and the calls of the night birds. Once he heard a dingo howl and he worried about a pack of dingoes attacking him whilst he was unable to escape or defend himself, but he never saw any. Gary would release him early in the morning and they would have something to eat. Then Gary would tell him he could sleep in the bed but, when he awoke, Gary was always sitting there, watching him, the rifle across his knee. At least it was still quite cool in the mornings and he would sleep fairly well.

He had no toothbrush and when he asked Gary if he had a spare one, he said to use his finger. It was better than nothing. He had no clean clothes to wear. He had to walk around in his underpants whilst his clothes dried – not that they took long in the heat. Then he'd put them back on and wash his undies. He also had to wash Gary's clothes, but Gary had a spare set, which made it easier. There was no shower, they had to wash themselves from water in the tin bowl and he had to ask Gary to take him outside to go to the toilet.

There wasn't much chance of escaping and, if he did manage it, he would have to follow the track to find his way back to the road and he knew that Gary would somehow manage to drive the car and probably shoot him down. By his calculations, they were about sixty kilometres from the main road and Gary would know that this was the only way he could go. He didn't know what there was further inland from here but it looked to be only bush and it didn't make much sense to try and find out on foot. He considered attacking Gary when he came close enough to put the handcuffs on and grabbing the key to the vehicle, but Gary was pretty wiry and David wasn't much of a fighter. He wasn't sure he could take him.

Chapter Seventeen
The Day They Met A Killer

Whilst he was handcuffed to the tree at night, David had plenty of time to reflect on their chance meeting with Gary. When he did manage to nod off, he relived that dreadful morning when Gary shot Jayden. He saw again Jayden's look of surprise, before he fell to the ground. He remembered what it felt like to drive away and leave Jayden lying there. He would wake up sweating and groaning. When he remembered where he was, he would realise that he was stiff and sore and shift his body to try to find a more comfortable position. Then his mind would start to work - had someone found Jayden's body by now? Was he still lying there in the open, all alone? How was he going to face Jayden's wife, Emma? Assuming he could escape from this nightmare. Jayden had been kind enough to agree to go into the outback with him. He didn't even know him very well, would not have called him a friend before their journey together. They played at the same Tennis Club and talked sometimes between matches. It was only when he had asked around at the Club if anyone was interested in taking a trip with him, that James Player, whom

David often partnered, had suggested he talk to Jayden because he knew that he had taken several trips in the outback with his wife. James had cautioned him to travel with someone who was experienced because of the dangers involved. He was sure James hadn't envisaged the sort of danger he now found himself in! Now, if he lived, he would have to see Emma and tell her how sorry he was that Jayden had died.

If only they hadn't gone to look at those rock drawings! When Jayden had mentioned that there was some Aboriginal art in the Blackdown Tableland National Park, quite close to where they were, he had jumped at the chance to see them. They had travelled as far as Longreach and Winton in Central Queensland. Between the two towns he had seen his first cattle drive. Jayden had been driving and they were rattling along at a good speed when David realised that all they could see up ahead was dust. A huge dust cloud seemed to be travelling towards them. Jayden slowed down. As they came closer to it, they could see cattle, lots of cattle. There must have been three or four hundred head, with four stockmen on horses and three Kelpie dogs. Jayden stopped the vehicle on the side of the road and they sat and waited for them to pass.

"I hope they don't knock my vehicle," Jayden commented.

"You must have come across them before, with all your travelling," David had said.

"Yes, but not actually on the road before. Usually, they are on a stock trail running alongside it."

"Might have come off a property round here somewhere and be heading for the trail," David suggested.

"Well, whatever, we have no choice in the matter. We have to sit tight here until they pass and hope they don't put any dents in it!"

It took a while for the cattle to work their way around the vehicle. The lead stockman touched his hat in acknowledgement as he went past and the dogs worked hard to keep the cattle through the narrower track. Although they had the windows closed, the dust from the sides of the road stirred up by the cattle found its way inside and they both coughed at regular intervals. Eventually the last stockman filed past them and they continued onwards.

In Longreach they visited the Stockman's Hall of Fame, dedicated to the stockmen and bushmen of the outback, which was interesting. They also visited the Qantas Museum, a tribute to Australia's national airline. Jayden had been inside them before but he said they were well worth another visit. There was plenty to see and it made a change from the outback scenery. In Winton, David had enjoyed seeing the dinosaur footprints. He had been fascinated; to think he was seeing proof of massive creatures which had lived on earth so many years ago! They visited the Dinosaur Museum as well as going to the dinosaur stampede area.

David had never seen any Aboriginal drawings and it seemed too good an opportunity to miss. Jayden told him that this particular National Park was only a small one and it wouldn't take them far out of the way on their journey home. They had arrived early in the morning and taken the Goon Goon Dhina cultural trail. It was only a couple of kilometres walk and at the end of the loop there was a rock overhang, where they had found the rock art handprints. To be honest, it wasn't that impressive, but David was still pleased to have seen them. On the way back, a large goanna crossed the track right in front of them. It didn't take much notice of them, stopping to fix them with a long stare, before ambling across the track at its own speed and disappearing into the bush. It was the biggest goanna David had ever seen, but Jayden said he had seen quite a few even bigger over the years.

They had returned to the vehicle and taken a long drink of water. They decided they might as well drive the loop road to Mitha Boongulla, whilst they were there. About half-way around, the back tyre on the passenger's side blew. Jayden reversed off the track and into the bush to change it. They hadn't seen anyone else on the track, but it was narrow and he didn't want to block it.

They had been standing at the back of the vehicle, chatting about the drawings, when another vehicle came along the track and parked not far away. The driver sat in the vehicle for a while, which they thought was odd. Jayden decided he should get on with changing the tyre. He put the jack under the slide-on camper and soon had the flat tyre lying on the ground beside him. I grabbed the spare and rolled it over the ground, glancing across at the other vehicle. Jayden, who was on the ground behind our camper, asked me what was happening, as his view was blocked.

"He opened the door again and now he's walking towards us," David had told him.

He looked to be in his thirties, thin and wiry, brown

hair, scruffy beard.

"How are you going?" he asked. "Do you need a hand?"

"G'day, mate," Jayden had replied. "No, we're okay, thanks. I've nearly got this spare on."

"Anything worth seeing here?"

They told him about the drawings and he seemed chatty and friendly. He asked them where they had been and they told him that they had been to Emerald and around that area.

"Find any gems?" he had asked.

"Not enough to retire on!" David had replied.

"We went as far as Barcaldine, now we're heading for home." Jayden said.

"What about you?" Jayden had inquired.

"Just kind of cruising around," was all the reply he received. He said his name was Gary and they introduced themselves. Then he said goodbye and returned to his vehicle. Jayden finished tightening the nuts on the wheel and pushed the flat tyre to the back of the vehicle, when his head jerked up and he looked at something behind David.

"Easy there, mate. What's going on?" Jayden asked.

David turned around to see Gary coming up behind

him, armed with a rifle.

"Think I might relieve you of those gemstones you found," Gary said, pointing the rifle at Jayden.

"Okay, if you need them that bad," Jayden replied, giving David a nod that he took to mean it seemed the best thing to do in the circumstances.

David looked around. There was not another soul, they were alone in the bush with this man with a rifle. It seemed they didn't have much choice but to hand over the gems. David reached into the back of the vehicle and, after shuffling a few things, brought out the small cloth bag which held their meagre find. They had decided to put the gems together when they took them to be valued in Rubyvale and hadn't bothered to split them again. David wished they had, because he might have been able to keep the sapphire he had been planning to have made into a ring for Sandra. David took a step forward and handed the gems to Gary. At the same time, Jayden must have reached across and grabbed the wheel brace, but Gary saw him. That's when he fired the shot. Jayden fell backwards, a neat bullet hole in his forehead.

Sandra would be wondering where he was by now.

How long before she alerted the authorities that he was missing? He didn't think it would be long, as she hadn't heard from him for days.

He must have nodded off for a while, because he was woken by Gary ranting and raving.

His foot must have gone septic, David thought. *Great, if I can't get him to come and undo these handcuffs I'm going to be stuck here until I die of thirst and he'll probably die inside the hut.*

"Gary, mate, you've got to come and undo these handcuffs," David yelled. "Gary, can you hear me?"

Silence. He tried again. "Come on Gary, take these handcuffs off and I'll make some coffee."

Gary limped out of the hut, using the rifle as a crutch. He had taken the bandage off his foot and David could see it looked red and angry.

"Your foot's gone septic. Come and undo these handcuffs and I'll have a look at it."

Gary eyes looked wild and nearly as red as his foot.

"Come on, mate. Get these off me."

Gary fumbled in his pocket for the key and staggered over to David. He had difficulty holding the key still and David was worried he would lose his temper and throw it in the bush.

"Just take your time, Gary. Undo these and I'll put the kettle on."

David sighed with relief when the handcuffs sprung free. Gary lent on him as they walked the few steps back to the hut, still keeping a good hold on the rifle. David unloaded him on to a chair and put the kettle on. Then he turned the other chair around so that Gary could put his foot up on it. David took a look at it and didn't like what he saw.

"Not looking good, mate. You need some antibiotics - or you might lose the foot," David added, in an attempt to frighten him. He didn't need to feel Gary's forehead to know that he was consumed by fever.

Gary started raging again. After a few minutes, he said "No doctors, no antibiotics. You stuffed up my foot – you can fix it."

"You're burning up. You've got a fever." David thought hard for a few moments. He needed to come up with something. "We'll soak the foot in some warm water and salt, see if that helps."

David poured hot water out of the kettle into the tin bowl and added a liberal dose of salt and a small amount of cold water. He deliberately left it very hot. Gary cringed when he put his foot in the bowl, but kept it there.

"We'll soak it every couple of hours and see how it goes. Or I could drive you into town to a doctor."

"No doctor," Gary replied through gritted teeth.

David kept up the salt and hot water treatment every couple of hours and Gary soaked his foot for half-an-hour at a time. The foot was certainly clean after a couple of soaks and, by evening, David thought it looked a little less puffy. Gary had taken several painkillers but he was still feverish. David began to think he was going to have a chance of escaping. In his drowsy state, there was a good chance Gary would fall asleep without remembering to put the handcuffs on. All David needed to do was to slip the car key out of Gary's pocket and take off in the Toyota. He'd take a chance now and try to wrestle the key off him, if Gary didn't have that rifle lying under his arm on the far side of the bed, next to the wall. In Gary's weakened state, it wouldn't be as hard to overcome him, but David had seen how quickly he could pull the trigger. Still, if he crept up to him, by the time Gary realised what was happening and pulled the rifle up to aim, David could be on top of him. Sooner or later, he was going to have to make a move.

"Don't even think about it," Gary said, as if he had read his mind. He pushed himself up to a sitting position. "See this?" He pulled out a flick knife from his right-hand pocket. "If I don't get you with the rifle, I'll stick you with this." He managed an evil grin, his yellow teeth making it seem all the more deadly. "Come over here and give me your right arm." He slipped the handcuffs back on to David's right wrist, then told him to lie down beside the bed, facing his feet. Leaning over, he handcuffed him to the bottom of the iron bed, before lying back down and falling asleep. David wondered about grabbing hold of Gary with his left hand, but he could only reach his feet and that would only get him shot.

David must have dropped off in this uncomfortable position because he was woken by Gary getting out of bed. He hobbled to the table and grabbed the painkillers.

"We got any more of these?" he asked.

"Yes, I bought four boxes."

Within a couple of days Gary was feeling better. The salt water had reduced the swelling in the foot and he had found a box of paracetamol in the cupboard. It was well out-of-date, but it reduced his fever. His knee was swollen and painful too, but that was to be expected for a few days. As long as nothing had been permanently damaged it would gradually improve, David assured him. Since handcuffing David to the leg of the iron bed that day, Gary had continued to handcuff him to the bed at night, instead of the tree, which was a bit of an improvement. The downside to that was that he also handcuffed him to the bed leg when it was his turn to sleep in the bed.

"How long are we going to stay in this hut?" David asked Gary on the fourth day.

"Until I say so."

On the sixth day, Gary's foot started to swell again and this time the salt water baths didn't relieve it.

"I think you've got a deep-seated infection in your foot," David announced after inspecting it. "I don't think the toe I straightened is properly seated either. Between that and the smashed big toe, it's pulling it apart all the time. It's a mess."

Gary swallowed the last two pain killers in the packet.

"How many more of these have we got?" he asked.

"That's it. The last one."

"Doesn't matter, I've got a plan. You can heat me up

some soup and then we'll get going."

"Going where?"

"To a mate of mine. He's a doctor. He'll fix me up."

David was glad to be out of the hut and back on the road, even if he didn't know where, or to what, he was headed. He let out a sigh of relief when he saw the main road ahead of him.

"Go left," Gary instructed.

They turned left and headed north. When the first petrol station came into view, Gary demanded that David pull in and buy some more painkillers. Once again, he didn't proffer any money. David checked his wallet. He had enough to pay cash this time, but he was not going to have much money left.

"I could pay with my card. That would leave us this cash," he suggested.

"So that someone can track where you are? I don't think so. Use the cash. No funny business, either. And get us something to eat."

David did his best to engage eye contact with the cashier, but he was busy making coffee for another customer. David picked up the pain-killers, a loaf of bread and a bottle of Coke and ordered four pies. Next, he tried eye-balling the other customer, but he was busy reading the newspaper headlines. When David paid, the cashier was talking to someone else. Frustrated, he returned to Gary and handed him the pain-killers. Then he took the two water containers and filled them at the tap. No-one came near him whilst he waited.

Gary was on his phone when he returned.

"Thanks mate, I'll owe you. Yes, we'll be there tomorrow morning." He hung up and turned to face David.

"You can eat and drive at the same time, can't you?" Gary demanded when David sat at the wheel, eating one of the pies.

David turned the key and drove back on to the highway. Gary passed him the bottle of Coke and he took a long drink, before eating a second pie. The scenery hadn't changed much - dry bush, sparse and uninteresting in a flat landscape. David wished once again that he had been able to grab his own phone from the dashboard before getting into Gary's vehicle. Not that there was any phone reception at the hut where they had been, of course, but he might have had a chance to use it at some stage. Then he realised it would probably have a flat battery by now anyway.

When the sun started to drop in the sky, Gary instructed David to turn off the highway down a minor road. A few kilometres along, he pointed to a clearing and David drove in.

"Make some coffee. We'll have some of that bread and one of those tins of corned meat."

David spent another uncomfortable night handcuffed to the steering wheel. Tired and stiff by morning, he made coffee as soon as he was released, relieving himself behind the vehicle whilst the camp stove boiled the water.

"Not far now," Gary offered whilst they ate. "We turn off up here a bit and then cross the river."

A couple of hours later they crossed the river via a low bridge.

"Does this river flood?" David asked, making conversation.

"Sometimes. Not very high now though."

"Does your mate live on a property?"

"Yes. Nice place, quiet. Bit run down, last time I was there."

It was the most Gary had spoken in the last few days.

Chapter Eighteen
Outback Hell

David drove along a country road for almost forty kilometres before Gary told him to cross a creek and take a narrow track off to the left.   It led to a typical, sprawling, country house, built of fibro sheeting and painted blue. The house had a wrap-around verandah, a bare front yard and a couple of outbuildings to one side. It had an air of general neglect; rotting fences, weeds growing around the verandah posts, overgrown bushes. The paint was peeling off the front door and the painted walls were badly faded. There were no neighbours in sight and David wondered how far he would have to walk to find help. He was already hopeful that he might be able to make an escape whilst the doctor was tending to Gary's foot. He was aware that, ideally, he needed a vehicle but, by now, he was willing to take any chance of escape.

An overweight man in shorts and a T-shirt opened the front door as Gary manoeuvred himself out of the vehicle. Standing around five foot ten inches tall, his short, ginger hair stood on end and he bore several days stubble on his chin. Not that David could comment, he had a fair growth himself by now. The man watched as Gary hobbled towards him and made his way up the three steps to the front door.

"Good to see you, mate," he said as they shook hands. "Looks as if you've got yourself in a fine mess."

"All thanks to him," Gary replied, nodding his head in disdain, at David. "Smashed my foot up with a wheel brace."

"You didn't do anything to make him mad, I suppose?"

Gary ignored the barb and pushed past him.

"Let me take the rifle."

"Not likely. That's all that keeps him with me. I need him to drive me. Makes himself useful too. His name's David."

"Harry," the man said and proffered his hand as David came up the steps. They shook and he stepped back to let David enter.

The man who was going to fix Gary's foot looked David up and down, with blue eyes that protruded too far out of their eye sockets. He had the reddened nose of a heavy drinker and bushy eyebrows that hadn't been trimmed for a long while, if ever. David knew that he looked dishevelled himself, his clothes rumpled and he'd neither shaved, combed his hair or cleaned his teeth properly since Gary had abducted him.

"Looks pretty harmless to me," Harry commented wryly to Gary. "Anyway, you won't need the rifle here. Where's he going to run to? You know as well as I do there's nothing around here. As long as you hang on to the car keys and I hang on to mine. There's a room out the back, where you can lock him up, if you want. Where did you pick him up?"

"That's another story. Might tell you later."

Harry led them down the passageway to the kitchen and made a point of picking up his keys from the table and putting them in his trouser pocket. David thought being locked in a room would be a big improvement to being handcuffed to a tree or a bed. Perhaps he could break out of it whilst they were asleep.

"All right. I'll make you a cup of coffee and then I'll take a look at that foot of yours."

The house was messy, but its owner cleared a space at the table and they sat around and drank big mugs of coffee. Afterwards he showed Gary and David a room at the back of the house. There was a sliding bolt across the outside of the door.

"He won't come to any harm in here," Harry, said.

210

"There's only a slit of a window and that's nearly in the roof."

Gary nodded and David obligingly walked into the room. There was a single bed, a small bedside table and an old brown armchair. He heard the bolt slide behind him. He sunk into the chair; it was the most comfortable he had been for days. The men walked back into the interior of the house, but a few minutes later, David heard footsteps returning. The bolt was slid open and Harry handed him a bucket.

"Don't want you making a mess in there."

David took the bucket and sighed. He could see he was going to be stuck here for a while. The window was very narrow, but maybe at a pinch he might push himself through it. Then he realised dejectedly that, even if he pushed the bed under the window, he still wouldn't be able to reach it.

He heard Harry telling Gary to put his foot up on a stool and knew Harry was examining it.

"You're right, it's not looking good, Gary. I'm going to wash it and put some antiseptic cream on it for now. You know you should go to a hospital and have it fixed up properly."

"I can't go to a hospital, you know that. That's why I

came to you."

"Okay, it's your foot. Tomorrow, I'll do something with it. I'll have a think about it and see what I've got here that I can use."

David lay down on the single bed and fell asleep almost immediately.

It was dark when he awoke. There was some light coming under the door, sufficient for him to see a light switch on the wall, which he turned on. He was hungry now and hoped that Harry would feed him. He didn't have to wait long before he heard footsteps and the bolt slid back. Harry opened the door, holding a cup of tea and a bowl of stew.

"You're awake then? Your food's gone cold, but you probably won't care."

He put a large plate of food on the floor and locked the door. David pounced on the stew. It wasn't quite cold and it had plenty of meat of some description, as well as vegetables. The tea was hot and he wolfed down the best meal he had eaten in days. He had hoped that he would be allowed out of the room to eat with Harry and Gary but it was beginning to look as if he was going to remain a prisoner in this back room. He couldn't hope to escape if he couldn't get out of it.

Sinking into the luxury of a proper bed, basic though it was, David had the best night's sleep since his capture. The iron camp bed in the hut had been okay, but this one had a good mattress. The next morning, he felt revitalised and ready to plan his getaway. Harry unlocked the door not long after he woke and told him to take his bucket and empty it in the toilet in the bathroom and to have a shower. He had to put his dirty clothes back on afterwards, but he still felt better. When he had finished Gary motioned with the rifle for him to go back in the room, where he found a plate of bacon and eggs and a cup of strong coffee. As Harry closed the door to the room, he told him he was going to see what he could do about fixing Gary's foot this morning, so David was to stay quiet.

David enjoyed his bacon and eggs and took his time over his coffee. A little later he heard Gary scream out in pain. *Good,* he thought, *I hope it hurts like hell.* He heard Harry apologise and say that he would give Gary a couple of injections in the foot to numb it. Over the next hour or so he could hear sounds of what, he assumed, were instruments being picked up and put down on the kitchen table and a couple of mild curses from Harry. He heard Gary ask if Harry was going to be able to fix his foot and Harry replied that he would do the best he could, but that Gary should go to a hospital and have it fixed properly.

"Never mind hospitals and doctors. You're a doctor and you owe me big time from that time in the Northern Territory."

"De-registered doctor," Harry corrected him. "I haven't forgotten, Gary. That's why I'm doing what I can, but I'm not an orthopaedic surgeon you know!"

So, David mused, these two had some history and it sounded as if they had been involved in something illegal in the past. De-registered doctor or not, he couldn't assume that Harry would help him to get away from Gary. He was going to have to come up with something himself. At least after two good meals he was beginning to feel up to the task.

David looked around the room again. If he balanced the chair on top of the bed, maybe he could reach the window. He lifted the chair on to the bed, but it was obvious he still wasn't going to reach the window. The ceiling was at least twelve foot high and the bed was very low – he would still be a couple of feet short. He took the chair down off the bed and sat on it; he needed another plan. He thought about standing behind the door next time Harry opened it and catching him off-guard, but Harry was fairly solid and wouldn't be easy to push out of the way. He didn't know if Gary would be sitting in a chair with his rifle ready to shoot him. Perhaps he would go to sleep after Harry had finished working on his foot, but maybe he would be sitting up with a drink in one hand and his weapon close by. He knew Gary wouldn't hesitate to shoot him, to stop him escaping. He wouldn't want him going to the police. In fact, the more he thought about it, he couldn't see a good outcome. How could Gary let him go, knowing he was going to report Jayden's death to the police, and his own kidnapping? How could he convince Gary that he would not? No, there was only one way he was going to get out of this alive and that was to escape. But how? He couldn't even escape from this room.

"All finished," Harry announced a short while later. "I've done my best. You're going to have to make sure it doesn't get infected. I've re-set three toes and stitched the skin together where it was split. I think you've got a couple of small broken bones inside your foot, but there's nothing I can do about them. I've got a pair of crutches you can have. I've got a couple of proper boots here too, somewhere."

David could hear Harry moving things around.

"Here they are. Mmm. Not going to be much use to you though, much too small. I've got some plaster of Paris, but I can't use that either, not with the open wound. You'll have to keep the foot up, keep the weight off it for six weeks and see how it is at the end of that time. It's never going to be as good as it was and you might still have to see an orthopaedic surgeon."

"Thanks, mate. I appreciate it. What about my knee? Is anything broken?"

"It's too swollen to tell at the moment. I don't think the kneecap is out of place but it looks like you took a hell of a whack."

"You can say that again. The swelling had gone down quite a lot, but hobbling around on it has set it off again."

"I'll give you some pain killers to take with you. They're strong ones, mind, so go easy on them."

"Perhaps we could stay here for a couple of days? Until my foot settles down?" Gary wheedled.

Harry didn't reply straight away; he obviously had some reservations about having Gary hanging around.

"I guess so," he replied after a minute or two. "Only

two days though, then you'll have to get going. I don't want any part of whatever's going on with David."

"Sure. I'll be right by then. David's helping me out for a bit, that's all."

"Then why you've got him locked up?"

"Ah, well. He might want to shoot through on me and I need him around for a while longer."

The rest of the day dragged for David. Harry brought him a sandwich at lunchtime and another cup of coffee. At least he was being well fed. David knew that his only chance was going to be to surprise Harry when he brought him food, but he could never be sure where Gary was and he didn't want to run straight into his rifle. He needed to wait until Gary went for a lie-down and then rush Harry when he opened the door.

The weather in the outback was decidedly hot now, not pleasantly warm as it was when he and Jayden had started their trip. Sweat dripped off him and his trousers were sticking to him. The room was hot and stuffy and the back of his hair was wet, as if he'd stepped out of the shower. He called out, through the door.

"Hey, Harry. Have you got a fan I can have? It's hot as hell in here."

"What do you think this is, the Ritz?"

David listened, hoping to hear the sound of footsteps bringing him a fan, but there was no movement. He lay down on the bed and stared at the ceiling. Perhaps Harry would go out at some stage and then he could call Gary in on some pretence and push past him. No, that was too risky, Gary was bound to have his rifle with him. Even if he didn't shoot him, he'd probably hit him with the butt and knock him out. Still, he did have the bucket as a weapon. It was made of steel, not plastic, and if he threw the contents over Harry or Gary and maybe hit them on the head with it, he would have the advantage.

Nightfall finally came and the temperature dropped. David thought about trying to escape when Harry brought his him dinner, but he knew it would be hopeless trying to get away in the dark. He would have cover – once he was away from the house, they'd never find him - but he didn't fancy his chances of finding his way back to the road, without following the track. That was the first place they would look for him. They'd have the car headlights and maybe even a torch. He needed to get the keys to one of the vehicles if he was to have any chance of getting away.

In the night it started to rain – large, heavy drops,

followed by thunder and lightening and then a deluge of water, which kept David awake for most of the night. The tin roof made it sound worse, like hail battering down. He finally dropped off to sleep in the early hours and awoke to hear the rain still pouring down outside. Harry brought him his breakfast not long after he had moved to sit on the chair.

"I thought it didn't rain at this time of year," David said when the door opened.

"It doesn't usually, but we do have storms like this, occasionally. It will fill the water tank up, which will be great."

Harry put the tray with eggs on toast and coffee on the edge of the bed and backed out of the room without another word. David ate his breakfast and then stretched out on the bed. It was going to be another long day. He wondered what Sandra was doing. Did she think he was dead? Had anyone found Jayden's body? If they had, the police would be searching for him. They would have found his phone inside the vehicle. That thought was comforting, but he couldn't imagine anyone would find him out here, it was too isolated. He thought about his daughters, Avril and Bethany. Were they missing him? He often went away on business trips.

Maybe they thought he was delayed with work. Sandra wouldn't want them to worry, but she must be nearly out of her mind. He selfishly hoped she was missing him as much as he was missing her.

His mind turned to when they met, on a cruise from Sydney to London. His girlfriend at the time, Isobel, had recently broken up with him and he had taken the cruise on the spur of the moment, hoping she would miss him and welcome him back. He had met Sandra on the cruise and danced with her nearly every night. He liked her straight away; she was down-to-earth, funny, full of life, but he still had hopes of being reunited with Isobel and didn't take things any further. He thought that suited Sandra anyway. She had been divorced for two years, but was still very angry with her ex-husband over his infidelity and seemed very wary of getting too close to anyone. They had a lot of fun and at the end of the cruise, went their separate ways. When he discovered that Isobel had already met someone else and had moved on, he was devastated. Time has a way of healing wounds of the heart and eventually he realised that he was ready to move on himself. That's when his thoughts kept returning to Sandra, her large green eyes and her flaming red hair. He had to admit that he had also been attracted to her very curvaceous figure. He started dating again, but no-one he met held his interest. In the end, he decided to try to find Sandra. Fortunately, she had mentioned the firm where she worked and he contacted them to see if she was still working there. She had been surprised to hear from him, but not unhappy, and had agreed to go out to dinner with him. They took it slowly at first, but it soon became apparent that they had a lot in common apart from dancing. When they admitted to each other that this could be serious, their love exploded.

David sighed. He would give anything to be back in Glenhaven with them. Why had he decided, at his age, that he should see the outback? If he was honest, there wasn't much to see anyway – a few scrubby trees, lots of dirt, some kangaroos. They did see a few emus. There were fifteen, including some babies, walking alongside the road, near Longreach. Mostly emus kept out of the towns, but in times of drought, Jayden told him, they would walk down the main streets looking for food. No, the outback wasn't for him, he had decided, which was probably why he hadn't wanted to explore it beforehand. Jayden saw it differently, he loved the wide, open spaces and the red soil. David knew that he belonged in the suburbs of Sydney, with his family. He was pulled from his thoughts by the sound of a strange voice talking and he realised Harry must have turned on a radio. He listened carefully to a news report. There had been a murder in Brisbane and a knifing on the Gold Coast.

"I only put the radio on to hear the weather report!" Harry commented. "If it's raining like this upstream, we'll be flooded in. The creek divides not far from here and this house sits in the middle. We'll be trapped here for days."

"Not a problem. My foot needs time to heal."

Harry snorted and turned the radio back on. They had missed the weather section but he searched for a weather station and eventually found one. The news wasn't comforting, with reports of considerably more rain in their area.

"That's it then. The creek will already be in flood by now and with the extra water coming from the river upstream, it won't be going down too soon."

"Will the house flood?"

"No, it stays dry, it's high enough, but the track's impassable in a vehicle. You couldn't even cross the creek on foot. There's no-one else around here and the road's forty-five kilometres away."

Harry grabbed a Driza-Bone jacket and a hat from a hook near the door.

"I'll go and take a look at the creek and see how high it is."

Harry returned a few minutes later and David heard him shaking the rain off his coat.

"Well?" asked Gary.

"It's already in flood alright, both sides. You won't be going anywhere for a few days. What did I do to deserve being stuck with you and your mate?"

"You weren't exactly an innocent party in the Northern Territory. Don't forget it was me who pulled you out of that mess."

"What a mess it was too! Talk about a robbery gone wrong. You said it was a push-over. The jeweller was an old man, wouldn't give us any trouble."

"How was I to know he'd fought in two wars and kept a gun under the counter! You're lucky I saw him reach for something and pushed you out of the way. Saved your life, as I remember."

"You didn't have to shoot him! We could have made a run for it. You killed him with a bullet through the chest. Then you killed the young girl who came out from

223

the back room!"

"He wasn't the only one who'd fought in a war and the girl was screaming; someone would have heard."

"Someone took the number-plate of your car. They knew who they were looking for, even though you stole another car and left yours behind. Fortunately for me, no-one was able to get a good description of me, but your Driver's Licence photo was flashed around everywhere."

David heard Gary grunt and the sound of the kettle starting to boil.

"That's why I've been in the bush ever since."

There was silence as the two men drank their tea. David heard their cups being rinsed and left on the sink to dry.

"Might as well let David out of that room," Harry said. "He can't go anywhere whilst the creek is flooded. He can make himself useful around here."

"Better make sure there are no knives or other weapons around. We don't want him attacking us," Gary observed.

"Does he look like the type to attack anyone? He's a city boy – a pen pusher!" Harry replied with contempt. "You worry about hanging on to your rifle."

Chapter Nineteen
Flooded In

Now he knew now why Gary wouldn't go near a hospital. David had wondered if Gary had murdered anyone else. Three people was enough, he supposed. Four, if he killed him. David didn't think that Gary would have any qualms about making it four. He didn't want to dwell on that. It looked unlikely that he was going to be able to escape for a few days now, if the creek was impassable.

For the next three days David was given the run of the house. It was a welcome change from being locked in the room, even if he was still locked in the room at night. The rain stopped on the second day and he was even allowed to wander around outside. He walked down to the creek, which wrapped itself around the property and he saw how high and fast-moving the water was – there was no point in even considering trying to cross it now. David decided his best chance would come when the water started to recede. If he could get the keys to one of the vehicles when the creek first became passable, he could get away. The problem was that both Harry and Gary seemed to keep their keys in their pockets at all times and he suspected they even slept with them.

By the next day, David had another plan. If he left the house as soon as the creek water started to drop, they would assume that he had managed to cross the creek and had headed for the road. If he could find somewhere to hide out for a few hours until they had searched for him, given up and returned to the house, he might have a chance to escape. He could follow the track to where it joined the road. They wouldn't expect him to stay anywhere close to the house, they would assume he had headed for the road. He found a clump of trees and bushes about four hundred metres from the house and worked out that the best place to cross the creek was a hundred or so metres towards the house. The creek seemed narrower there and, once the water slowed down, he reckoned he could make it. He'd probably be soaking wet, unfortunately, but he couldn't wait for the creek to go down too far or he'd be locked up in that small room again.

The decision was made for him when Harry announced over dinner that the creek had started to drop and he would try to drive across the creek the next day. They needed supplies, he said, his chest-freezer was empty. He could probably shoot a couple of rabbits

226

but he'd prefer to drive the fifty-odd kilometres to the nearest store and stock up properly.

"Not that I'll need much for you guys now," he declared. "Once the creek's gone down another couple of inches you'll get your vehicle, Gary. Your foot will have healed enough for you to hobble to it!" He laughed, obviously pleased by the thought that they would soon be leaving.

David didn't get much sleep that night. He was too busy thinking about the best way to escape. Did he wait for Harry to drive away and then try to get Gary's car keys? Or did he cross the creek and head off along the track, knowing it would be some time before Harry came back? He would hear the vehicle coming from a long way off and could hide himself in the bushes. By the time Harry got back to the house and Gary told him what had happened, he could be quite a way along the track. Would Gary insist that Harry drive back to find him, or would Harry tell him to let the man go and force Gary to leave, driving with his bad foot? No, either way, that was too risky: He liked his other plan better. He'd wait until Harry left and then he'd hide in the clump of bushes he had picked out. He'd stay hidden there until they had given up looking for him and he'd cross the creek as soon as it was dark.

If David had thought about his plan for a little while longer, he might have been prepared for what happened next. After breakfast he cleared the dishes, as usual and washed and dried them. Harry walked down to the creek and came back to announce that he thought he could cross the creek without any problem and would try now to go and buy some food. He took the car keys out of his pocket then stopped and turned to David.

"I'll have to lock you up again. The creek is going down quickly."

David froze. If he allowed Harry to lock him up in the room again, he wouldn't be able to escape. Why hadn't he considered that Harry would lock him up again? He walked towards Harry as if he was going back to the room. He knew Gary was in the bathroom. Without thinking much about it, he stepped closer to Harry and kneed him in the groin. Taken by surprise, Harry doubled over. David brought his hand down over Harry's hand in a karate-style chop he had seen on TV, which knocked the car keys out of his hand. Swooping down on them, David took his chance and ran for the vehicle. He opened the driver's door, jumped in and turned the key in the ignition. The old vehicle spluttered and tried to burst into life, but it had been out in the rain and was still damp. It petered out and David turned the key again. This time it almost caught. One more time, David thought, but before he could turn the key again, the door opened and Harry hauled him out. Throwing punches wildly, David turned and tried to pull away, but he only succeeded in knocking Harry off balance. Harry fell, taking David with him and somehow managed to land on top of David, with most of his considerable weight on top of David's right leg. There was a sharp crack and David cried out in pain. He knew his ankle was broken. His flight for freedom was over.

Harry pushed himself up dusted himself off.

"Why did you go and pull a stunt like that?" he asked in disbelief.

David was in too much pain to respond. He rolled over, grimacing. Harry held out his hand and pulled him to his feet.

"What's going on out here?" Gary called out from the top of the steps. He had the rifle pointing right at them.

"It's nothing," Harry called back. "Bit of a misunderstanding, that's all."

Taking a firm hold on David's arm, he helped him to hop inside.

"Hold on to the table a minute, while I clear it," he instructed David, as he moved plates and coffee cups to the sink. "Okay, now lie yourself down on it."

The table had been roughly made out of wood a long while ago, but it was strong and sturdy. David eased himself on to it and Harry felt around David's ankle, confirming that it was broken. It was already starting to swell.

Gary watched; his rifle still trained on David. "What happened?" he demanded to know.

"David and I got a big tangled up, that's all. I lost my balance and fell on him. He's hurt his ankle. You can put that rifle down. He's not going anywhere now."

Gary watched whilst Harry fetched the plaster-of-Paris.

"Fortunately, I think it's a clean break, because I couldn't operate on it. Ankles can be tricky things. Once the swelling goes down, I'll set it in plaster of Paris and you'll have to stay off it for a while. If it hasn't improved in about three weeks, get yourself to a hospital where they can x-ray it."

Not much chance of that, David thought, the way things were going.

"Thanks, Harry."

"I'm disappointed you tried to make a break for it," Gary piped up, realising what had happened. "I thought you and me were mates."

David ignored the comment and watched as Harry put a teacloth filled with ice around his ankle.

"Stay there for a while until it settles down."

David lay back on the table and closed his eyes.

"You'll have to share the crutches – one each," Harry declared, taking one of Gary's crutches and handing it to David.

Later, when Gary was in the bathroom, Harry handed David some painkillers for the night.

"That was a stupid thing to do, David. If Gary had come out sooner, he'd have had no hesitation in shooting you."

"What do you think he is going to do anyway? You don't seriously think he is going to let me go, do you?" David replied, agitated. "I saw him shoot my mate, in cold blood. He's kidnapped me at gunpoint and kept me handcuffed and threatened with that rifle for days. As soon as I'm no further use to me, he's going to kill me, I know too much – and that day isn't going to be very far off. Another few days, he'll be able to drive himself."

"Nothing to do with me!" Harry replied, putting his hands in the air. "I let the two of you stay here for a few days, that's all. I even tried to fix you both up. I want you both gone, now, so I can get back to my peaceful life. I didn't buy a place all the way out here to have these sorts of problems."

"You've got to help me get away!" David pleaded. "Leave your car keys lying around for me. I'll leave the car for you to pick up at the main road – I can hitch a ride from there."

"Sorry, mate, it's not going to happen. I know what a temper Gary has; I know him from way-back. If I let you go, he's likely to shoot me!"

"We can make it look like you had nothing to do with it. Think about it, that's all I'm asking. Surely you don't want my death on your conscience?"

When Harry didn't answer, David took a couple of the painkillers and made his way slowly to his room. He heard the bolt slide across behind him and knew his attempt at appealing to Harry's better nature had failed.

Chapter Twenty
A Change of Luck

"Police are searching for David Pearson who, it is alleged, is missing from the site of a murder. Jayden Watson was found dead behind his vehicle at Blackdown Tableland National Park yesterday morning. Police have not said whether they think David Pearson may be responsible for the murder, or whether they think he was kidnapped by the killer - or killers. David is described as five foot eight inches tall, fifty-six years of age, dark hair worn short, brown eyes and a solid build. Anyone with any information should contact the police on..."

The radio was switched off in mid-sentence, but David had heard enough to know that Jayden's body had been found. Surely, they didn't seriously think he might have shot Jayden! It had never occurred to him that they might think he could be the killer. He had never even fired a gun. At least it meant that the police would be looking for him. He also realised that Harry was now aware of who he was and that there was no doubt that he had been kidnapped.

"Hell, Gary! Is this the David you've got locked up in my house? Please tell me that you didn't kill his mate and kidnap him?"

"Ah, well, let me explain..."

"Explain! I don't want the police coming here and finding him."

"They won't, Harry. Calm down. They're never going to come here looking for him. Anyway, I only need him until I've got the use of my foot again."

"Then what are you going to do? Drop him off at a train station so that he can tell the police what you did?"

David held his breath. This was where Gary was going to admit he was going to have to kill him.

"He won't talk. He'll be so pleased to be free that he'll keep quiet about all this."

Harry was quiet for a minute or two. "I wish I could believe you, Gary. I thought you'd have learned your lesson from that time in the Northern Territory."

"I didn't mean to kill his mate. I was relieving them of some gems they had found around Emerald and he went for the wheel brace. I shot one off and it was unlucky that it got him in the middle of his forehead. I hadn't aimed at him. He keeled over and that's when David picked up the wheel brace and smashed my foot. I think he was aiming for my head, but I moved too quick. I knew he'd done a lot of damage to my foot; it hurt like hell. While I was recovering, he hit me again, on the knee. I pointed the rifle at David and told him to get in the driver's seat of my vehicle and start driving. I didn't know for sure the other guy was dead," he lied.

"You didn't stop to help him either."

Gary was silent for a little while. "I've been living in the bush since I killed those couple of people in the Northern Territory. That's why I came to you for my foot. I've been hiding away. Suits me anyway, I like the quiet life in the bush."

"Well, you won't have any choice now. Did anyone see you driving out of the Park?"

"No, there was no-one around. The only one who knows I shot him is David."

"It sounds as if they may blame him for the murder. They don't seem to know what happened. You might be lucky – you could tell him you'll let him go if he takes the rap."

"Sure thing, Harry. He'll agree to anything to be set free."

Even David could hear the insincerity in Gary's voice. He was sure Gary didn't intend to let him walk away.

Later that morning, Harry checked David's ankle and declared the swelling had subsided. David watched as

Harry's large hands expertly wrapped some wet plaster-of Paris around his ankle. It felt cool and firm, but the ankle was still throbbing.

Two days later, David was woken by Gary's moans. He made his way out to the lounge, where Harry was already unbandaging Gary's foot.

"It's infected, Gary," he said as he pulled the last of the bandage from it. "That's why you are in so much pain. You need antibiotics."

"I soaked it in salt water last time it was infected," David informed him.

"I think it's beyond that now. Still, we'll try it – maybe it will ease it for a while. I'll go into town later."

David looked at the clock on the kitchen wall. It was only seven o'clock. Harry put a generous amount of salt in a container with some hot water and Gary soaked his foot in it. David made his way to the bathroom for a shower and, by the time he returned, Harry had set out three dishes and a box of cereal. He threw an old piece of cloth at Gary for him to dry his foot.

"We'll leave it uncovered for a while, let the air get to it." Harry said.

David glanced over at Gary's damaged foot. It was

swollen and angry-looking. He quickly looked away.

After they had eaten, Harry pulled on his boots.

"I'll go and see my doctor, make up some story. I'm pretty sure he'll give me some antibiotics you can take. I'll lock David in his room whilst I'm gone, that way you won't have to worry about him."

David didn't fancy spending the next few hours in that stuffy room.

"How about I come with you instead?" he suggested, hopefully.

"So that you can try and escape?" Gary asked incredulously.

"No, I'll behave. I don't fancy being stuck in that airless room in this heat, that's all."

"No chance, sorry," Harry replied.

"Oh, take him with you," Gary said, grimacing with pain. "Get him out of my sight, or I might do something rash, seeing how he caused this."

Harry thought for a moment. He didn't want to be the cause of David's death in his house but, on the other hand, he knew he was taking a chance if he took David with him. Someone might see him and recognise him, or he might try to escape.

"Take him!" Gary shouted. "Get him out of here.

There's a pair of handcuffs in my room, you can handcuff him to the steering wheel whilst you're at the doctor's. He's not going to run off, is he?"

To David's relief, Harry retrieved the handcuffs.

"Put them on so that his hands are behind his back. Then he won't trouble you whilst you are driving," Gary instructed.

David hobbled out to the car on his crutch, where Harry handcuffed him.

"You'll have to sit on the back seat, you'll never fit in the front one."

David positioned himself with his back leaning against the door, behind the passenger seat and stretched his legs across the seat.

It was very uncomfortable with his hands behind him and the rough track back to the road jarred David's ankle, but it felt good to be out of the house and away from Gary, who he thought was mad enough to open the door to his room and shoot him before Harry returned. He tried to make a mental note of the scenery as they drove. If he managed to escape it would be helpful to have some idea of where they were. It all looked much the same to him – scrub and dirt. It was better once they joined the road. It took three-quarters-of -an-hour before Harry slowed down and turned on to a side road. A short way down the track, David could see a group of three houses. Harry parked under a tree, behind the first house. Built of fibro, the faded-pink house had seen better days. Theirs was the only car and there was no-one else in sight. Any hopes David had of attracting someone's attention, whilst Harry was inside, were quickly evaporating. Still, you never knew, he might be lucky.

Harry lent over and undid one of the handcuffs, slipping it around and through the hole in the armrest. That left David in another awkward position.

"Won't be long," he said, marching up the steps to the back door and knocking loudly. A man, whom David thought was probably in his late fifties, opened the door and Harry walked inside. It obviously wasn't a very busy practice. Harry was only gone for ten minutes and no-one else drove in during that time. When he returned, Harry threw a paper bag on the passenger's seat and sat in the driver's seat.

"Aren't you going to take these handcuffs off the armrest?" David demanded.

"No, you're right until we get back home. I feel safer this way."

Approximately half-way back towards the house, Harry turned through a gate, down a well-used track. It led to a farmhouse, where Harry parked some distance away. At least he parked under a tree so David would have some shade.

"Won't be long," he said.

David watched him walk down the side to the back of the house. There was another car parked close to the farmhouse and he saw a middle-aged woman walk back to it with a parcel. She got in her car and drove out without even glancing his way. All the time he was waiting, David was willing someone else to drive in, in the hope he could attract their attention. Even if they didn't come over and help him, they may remember him later, if the police asked them. No-one else drove in and Harry soon returned with two large bags.

"That's the meat," he said as he put them on the passenger seat. "They sell fresh meat, a bit of bread and a few vegetables here. There's not much else around these parts."

"Where's the nearest large town?"

"Charters Towers, but that's a fair step from here."

"How do you know Gary?" David asked, anxious to make conversation and find out more about his kidnapper.

"We grew up in the same town, went to the same school. He was always trouble, even back then." Harry turned the radio on to a station which only seemed to have old seventies songs. It marked the end of their conversation.

In a couple of minutes, they were back on the road and heading back to Gary. David had enjoyed the outing, but he was no closer to freedom.

Gary's mood hadn't improved whilst they were away, but after a couple of days on the antibiotics, his foot started to respond. The redness and swelling was subsiding and he was able to put some weight on it again. The swelling on his knee had reduced quite a lot too, but David knew Gary was in pain whenever he put any weight on it. David was still very limited in how much he could move around too, so the days passed slowly, made more unbearable by the heat and the flies. They seemed to settle around his nose and eyes, were reluctant to be batted away and returned almost immediately. Harry was becoming less and less friendly as time passed and he was still stuck with his two unwanted guests. Occasionally he would borrow Gary's rifle and shoot a rabbit or even a wallaby for a change from tinned meat and soup. When he did that, David found himself locked inside the hot room again. Fortunately, Harry would let David out as soon as he returned, because it was unbearable to be inside the room during the day. David sat at the kitchen table and watched, fascinated, as Harry gutted the animal he had caught and removed its skin. He realised how his sheltered city-life had left him ill-prepared to survive alone in the outback.

Not long after Gary took the last of the antibiotics his foot started to swell again.

"Damn," Harry shouted, as he unwrapped it and surveyed the infection. "Those antibiotics didn't do much good. I'll never get rid of you two at this rate. I'll have to see if I can get something stronger. We need more food anyway."

Still dreaming of rescue, David again asked if he could go along for the ride. Again, Gary was keen to be rid of him and encouraged Harry to take him along.

"It's not like he's going to run off, with his ankle like that, is it?" he said.

With his hands handcuffed behind him, David leaned against the door, with his plastered ankle on the back seat. Surely this time, they would have to see someone.

There was one other car at the doctor's house, when they pulled in under the tree at the front. It was parked in the yard of the house next door, covered in dirt and dust and had obviously been driven for a long way on dirt tracks. Once again, Harry handcuffed David to the armrest. David looked around, wondering where the driver of the other car could be, but his hopes were dashed when Harry walked past it and glanced inside. The driver was stretched out fast asleep on the back seat. Harry pointed and grinned, before knocking on the doctor's door.

David moved around, trying to get comfortable. His right hip was aching and so was his ankle. The sound of a mobile phone ringing surprised him, especially when he realised it was coming from inside the car! Harry's phone must have slipped out of his pocket and was on the floor, under the seat. There was phone reception here! If only he could get hold of the phone, he could call Sandra. He turned on his stomach, so that he could reach under the seat, with his free hand. He winced as he twisted his broken ankle, flipping himself on to his stomach. He felt under the seat. The tips of his fingers found the phone, but it was out of reach. Frustrated, he let his left leg fall on to the floor, so that he was half-kneeling. He reached for the phone again and managed to get his fingers half-way along it. Carefully he pulled it towards him – he had it! He pushed himself back on to the seat and into a half-sitting position and dialled Sandra's number, praying for her to answer. The phone answered on the third ring.

"Sandra, it's me. Hello, sweetheart."

"David? David! Is it really you? Oh, my goodness, I've been so worried."

"I knew you would be. I'm so, so sorry."

"You're alive! Oh David, it is so good to hear your voice! I thought you were dead."

"Yes, I'm alive. You've heard about Jayden, I suppose?"

"Yes, we know he was shot. That's why we thought you were dead too."

"I knew you would be worried sick. I couldn't get to a phone. I was thinking about you all the time. It was the thought of you and the girls that kept me going. How are they? How are my Beth and Avril?"

"They're fine, truly. They will be so pleased to hear your voice though. They keep asking why Daddy hasn't rung."

"Listen, Sandra, I haven't got long. I've been

kidnapped."

"Kidnapped! Where are you?"

"I'm not too sure. Somewhere out the back of Belyando Crossing, in Queensland. Look, I'm using this bloke's phone and I'll have to hang up the minute he comes back. They've got me in an old house, way out of town, with no phone reception. It's near the Belyando River. I'm okay and I'm trying to escape, but I've broken my ankle, so I'm a bit limited in what I can do. The guy who kidnapped me, his name is Gary, and we're staying at the house of a de-registered doctor called Harry. Have you got that?"

"Yes, I'm going to contact the police as soon as we hang up."

"Good, darling. Tell them one of them has a rifle. Oops, got to go, he's on his way back. Love you."

David switched off the phone and threw it on to the front seat of the car, so that it slid down on to the floor, seconds before Harry opened the door. He was holding a paper bag, which presumably held the all-important antibiotics. He threw the bag on to the passenger's seat and looked around for his phone.

"Damn phone must have fallen out of my pocket. I'm

sure I had it when I left the house. Haven't seen it, have you?" he asked, giving David a quizzical look.

"No, Harry. I haven't seen it."

Harry felt around on the floor.

"Here it is. Thought I'd lost it." He looked from where he had found the phone, under the dashboard of the car, and to where David was lying. Deciding that there was no chance David could have reached it, he automatically looked to see if there were any messages and noticed the missed call. He hit redial and spoke to someone he called Phil. The conversation only lasted for a minute or two before he ended it. From what David gathered, Phil was inviting Harry to meet him at a pub in Charters Towers on Saturday week, but Harry declined, saying he was busy at the moment, maybe another time. He slipped the phone into his shirt pocket and positioned himself behind the wheel.

As they drove, David's thoughts were in a whirlwind. Would Sandra be able to give the police enough information for them to find him? If they stormed the house, would he be safe? He might be better to be locked in the room than in the lounge with the other two. He was petrified that Gary might shoot him, the only witness to Jayden's murder, especially if he thought he was responsible for the police arriving.

Harry pulled in at the farmhouse again and parked under the same tree as last time. Two cars drove in whilst he was waiting, but they drove straight up to the farmhouse door without looking his way. Harry returned with more food and a large case of bottled water and they were soon on their way back to the house. He could only hope that the police would rescue him soon.

Part Three

Chapter Twenty-One
Searching for a Kidnapper

Sandra put down the phone in disbelief. David was alive! She had almost given up hope of ever seeing him again. With shaky fingers, she dialled the number for Detective John Brady in Rockhampton and was relieved when he answered straight away. She explained to him that she had received a call from David, who was alive but said he had been kidnapped. She told him that her husband was being held in an isolated house, somewhere near Belyando Crossing, with a broken ankle. It wasn't much to go on, but Detective Brady assured her he would get some men out looking for him. It was going to be another time of waiting for Sandra.

Next, she rang Anna. Fortunately, Anna and Emma had already arrived at Blackall, so they had phone reception. After visiting Charleville, Anna didn't know why, but she felt they were moving further and further away from David. Nothing she could pin down, just a feeling that they were going the wrong way, so they had turned around and headed north again.

"Anna, you're not going to believe this, but I've had a phone call from David!"

"You have! Is he okay?

"He's broken his ankle, which is one of the reasons he hasn't been able to escape."

"Escape?"

"Yes, he said he's been kidnapped."

"Kidnapped? No wonder no-one has been able to find him. What happened? Do you have any idea where he is being held?"

"Somewhere near Belyando Crossing, he thinks." Sandra quickly filled me in on the limited information David had been able to give her.

"We're not that far from Belyando Crossing. We spent the night at Blackall. Emma's pointing to it on the map. She's saying we can probably get there in around six hours. We'll go and join the police in searching for him. Oh, Sandra, this is such great news. I wish I was there to dance around the lounge room with you!"

"So do I. I've missed you so much." I heard the break in her voice and knew she was struggling. "You don't have to go to Belyando Crossing, Anna," she said quietly. "You can come home now and let the police find him."

"Not a chance, Sandra. We've come this far, we'll see

it through to the end."

I could see Emma nodding her head in agreement.

"Thank you, Anna. You're a great friend. Please thank Emma for me too."

"I will. I'm going to give David a big hug from you! Now, you go and tell your parents and then let yourself have a good cry."

We took to the road again, driving towards Emerald. Emma was feeling stronger by now and had resumed her position behind the wheel. She drove all the way to Emerald. I was pleased to see our flyer was still on display in the caravan park and I brought the caravan park owner up-to-date with Jayden's death and the fact that David was alive, but still missing. She promised to contact us if David and his kidnapper came to the caravan park.

Next, I called in at the local radio station and spoke to Barry. He was excited by the new development and interviewed me over the radio. I explained to his listeners that we believed David Pearson had been kidnapped and was either still with Jayden's killer or stranded somewhere in the outback. Anyone who had seen anything suspicious was urged to contact the radio station. Barry promised to keep us updated if anyone called in with something useful.

We were not far from Beylando Crossing when I spotted a very old Kombie van pulled off the road and two young girls waving at us.

"Better stop and see what they want, we all help each other out here in the bush," Emma said. "Leave it to me to handle. You can't be too careful. There could be a couple of blokes hiding behind the van to ambush us."

I pulled over in front of them, which gave us the chance to look on the other side of the van. There was no-one else there. One of the girls ran up to Emma on the passenger's side. She was very young, probably no more than eighteen or nineteen.

"Thank you for stopping," she said. "We've run out of petrol. I know that's a stupid thing to do out here, but the petrol gauge doesn't seem to be very accurate."

"That's alright, love," Emma replied. "We can let you have some. How far are you going?"

"All the way to Cooktown! But if we could have enough petrol to get us to Beylando Crossing, that would be great. We'll pay you."

"No need. We've got plenty. Always happy to help out a fellow traveller."

Whilst Emma transferred some petrol from a jerry can to the Kombie van's tank, I got out for a stretch and talked to the girls.

"I'm Belinda and this is Lynn," the girl who had spoken to Emma said.

"I'm Anna and this is Emma," I told her. "That's a pretty old van you're driving."

"I know," Belinda replied, giggling. "It's all we could afford. We're here on holidays from England and some boys sold it to us at Brisbane airport. They said it went okay, they'd been up to the Northern Territory and back in it. They had done the same as us, coming out from the UK for a holiday and buying the van at the airport from some other tourists. We were told we wouldn't have any trouble selling it at the airport when we have finished with it."

I don't know much about cars, but it didn't look too great to me. It was full of rust and there wasn't much paint left on it. It must be thirty years old, at least. *These young tourists take a lot of chances*, I thought. There was no way I would have set out to travel around Australia in
it. Most of them had no idea how big Australia is or how rugged the landscape can be.

"Do you have water?" Emma asked, ever practical.

"Yes, thanks. One of the things the boys stressed was to carry lots of water."

"So now you know you also need to carry lots of petrol." Emma reminded them.

Before we left the girls, we showed them the photo of David and asked them if they had seen him. They shook their heads and I told them why we were looking for him. They took one of the posters and promised to keep a look out for him.

"So, you girls be careful," Emma warned them. "Not only to carry enough petrol and water but, remember, there's a killer on the loose out here somewhere."

Even the thought of a killer couldn't stifle the girls' enthusiasm. Thanking us again for the petrol, we waited until the Kombie fired up before we pulled back on to the road. For a few kilometres we could see them in our rear mirror, but the Kombie started to shake once they hit eighty kilometres an hour, they had told us, so we soon left them behind.

We arrived at Beylando Crossing late afternoon and parked outside the famous Roadhouse. It was a very basic building, not at all what I had been expecting for the only eating and refuelling stop for kilometres.

"Do you think we should contact Detective Brady, or what do you have in mind?" Emma asked me as we stretched ourselves.

"I was thinking that we'd go inside and have something to eat and chat to the owners. They may know where a certain de-registered doctor called Harry lives."

We ordered a couple of burgers and two beers. The Roadhouse was busy and obviously a regular stop for many travellers. After we had finished eating, I walked up to the counter.

"We're looking for an ex-doctor called Harry," I said to the middle-aged woman at the register. "He lives in quite an isolated spot somewhere near here, I believe."

"Sorry, love. I don't know him. As you can see, we are pretty isolated ourselves. There are a few bushies come in from time to time but I can't remember a Harry."

"Thanks. Do you think there is there anyone else here who might know?"

"You could try Jacko, over there," she replied, pointing to a man sitting alone at the end of the bar. "He's been around these parts a while."

We walked across to Jacko.

"Excuse me," Emma said. "Jacko, isn't it?"

A weather-beaten face turned towards us. Jacko had a long, grey beard which reached down to his chest and brown eyes that peered at us from under very bushy, grey eyebrows.

"What d'yer want?" he growled. Not one to be easily put off, Emma continued.

"We were wondering if you know an ex-doctor called Harry, who lives around here somewhere. We understand his place is pretty isolated and we're having trouble finding it."

"What do you want with him?"

"A friend of ours is staying with him. We have some news to pass on to him," Emma replied pleasantly.

"Never heard of him." Jacko turned back to his beer. We stood there for a couple of minutes, hoping he might turn his attention back to us, but he stared resolutely at his glass.

Disheartened we walked back to the vehicle and drove to the campground. It was nearly eight o'clock and any searching we were going to do would have to be done in daylight.

"Did you believe Jacko – that he doesn't know

Harry?" I asked as we drove away.

"I think so. It doesn't seem like Belyando Crossing is Harry's local shopping area," Emma replied.

"So, what are we going to do tomorrow?"

"We'll drive around a bit. We can ask where the nearest shops are from here. I think our best chance of finding Harry and David is by talking to someone where Harry goes regularly for petrol or food. We could drive around for ever and not find an isolated house in the outback."

I had to agree that Emma's suggestion was logical.

"We mustn't forget that David's kidnapper is probably the person who killed Jayden. We need to be very, very careful," I pointed out.

"What are the chances of us finding them when half the police force is out looking for them?" Emma retorted. "I hope they do find them before we do. I might want to exact some revenge otherwise."

The determined look on Emma's face worried me. I still didn't know whether she had brought a gun along with her. I hadn't seen any trace of one, but even so. Perhaps now was a good time to find out.

"Emma, do you have a gun with you?"

Emma turned to look at me, clearly annoyed.

"No, Anna, I don't. If we owned a gun, Jayden would have taken it with him. Maybe if he'd had a gun......."

"Okay, Emma, I wasn't sure, that's all. Now that I know we are unarmed, I'll be extra careful!" I said, trying to make a joke out of it.

We decided to have breakfast at the Roadhouse the next morning, so that we could ask a couple of the morning staff if they knew Harry and find out where the closest shops were located. There was a young girl on the till this morning and I asked her if she knew a retired doctor called Harry. Shaking her head, she said that she had only been working there for a couple of weeks. She suggested I ask another staff member, an older man in his sixties, who was clearing the tables.

"Excuse me," I said, intercepting him as he headed for the kitchen with an armful of plates.

He turned to face me, his eyes suggesting a heavy night of drinking the previous evening. I asked him if he knew where Harry, a retired doctor, lives. He told me tersely that he didn't know the man and hadn't seen him at the Roadhouse. I thanked him and returned to the more helpful girl on the till.

"Where are the closest shops to Belyando Crossing?"

I asked.

"Charters Towers. That's about two hundred kilometres north of here. Either that, or Clermont. Not much else around in these parts."

Disheartened, I returned to where Emma was sitting at a table, waiting for breakfast to arrive.

"There's nothing much else around here," I told her. "Charters Towers or Clermont seem to be the only options."

"There must be something in-between. Surely there's another roadhouse, or a petrol station selling supplies?"

We made a few more enquiries, but everyone confirmed there was no other stop between Clermont and Charters Towers.

"What do you think, Emma? Should we head towards Charters Towers or go back towards Clermont?"

"We've just come from Clermont, so I guess we go further north," Emma replied despondently. "If this Harry does his shopping at Charters Towers it's not likely anyone will know him, the place is too big. I thought there would be some type of corner shop where he would do his basic shopping but it doesn't seem as if there is one."

"Perhaps we should forget about the shop and

concentrate on checking out some of the tracks around Belyando. David definitely said he was being held somewhere close to the Crossing."

"That makes more sense. We'll fill up with petrol and fill the spare jerry cans too. We don't want to run out of petrol out in the bush, especially after lecturing those English girls!"

By the time the jerry cans had been filled I had come up with a better idea.

"We could spend days covering hundreds of tracks, Emma. Even if there is a house at the end of them, we're not going to be game to knock on the door. I'm going to ring Detective Brady and suggest they get some aerial surveillance out here. They can pinpoint the houses and the police can knock on the door."

Detective Brady answered his mobile phone after four or five rings – I was glad he had given me his direct number.

"Hi, Detective Brady. It's Anna Davies here. We're at Belyando Crossing. I was wondering if you could get some aerial surveillance here to track down some isolated houses."

'Now, why didn't I think of that?" he retorted sarcastically.

"Sorry, it's only because we haven't noticed any planes flying overhead."

"That's because I can't get a helicopter out here until tomorrow. Now, be a good girl and head for home. Leave the police work to the police."

Suitably chastised, I turned to see Emma watching me.

"He hung up on me! Says he's already arranged a helicopter for tomorrow. He told me to go home!"

Emma laughed. I was pleased to hear it; she had been so quiet.

"Oh well, what are we going to do now?"

"We should hang around here for another day and see if they find David. I'm sure you'll want to see him if they do. I definitely want to get a look at the man who killed my husband."

Emma worried me a little. I hoped she wasn't going to try anything silly.

It was a long day stuck at Belyando Crossing, with nothing to do. Emma wasn't worried. She was pleased to have internet connection and spent most of the day on her phone, playing games and looking at Facebook.

I spoke to Mike and Sandra, but other than telling

them that a helicopter was being brought in tomorrow, I didn't have much news and neither did they. Sandra was on tenterhooks, anxiously waiting for news of David, whilst at the same time, fearing for his safety until he was rescued. Mike was having problems at work with one of the programmes and working all hours to try and fix it. I don't think he even had time to miss me!

That evening we ate at the roadhouse again and I wandered amongst the tables showing diners a photo of David and asking them if they had seen him, or heard of a retired doctor named Harry who lived hereabouts. Nearly everyone was a traveller, passing through and no-one had seen David. I had thought we might see the English girls, Belinda and Lynn, at the roadhouse, but, since they were on a tight budget, they had probably made themselves something to eat in their van.

We heard the helicopter in the air about eight o'clock the next morning and watched it circling over Belyando Crossing. Next we watched as two police cars drove into town.

"Come on, Anna," Emma urged. "Get in, we're going to follow them."

"Are you mad?"

"No, we'll keep well back. They'll hardly know we are following them. They'll assume we're journalists, anyway."

I jumped into the passenger seat. Whilst I'd been on the phone to Mike this morning, Emma had already packed everything away. She took after the last police car like a dog after a rabbit. The police were guided by someone in the helicopter and soon headed up a track in the bush. Keeping a respectful distance, which wasn't hard as we tried to keep to the speed limit, we saw them pull up outside a small, neat home a few kilometres down the track. An old Holden car was parked outside. We pulled off to the side of the track about three hundred yards from the police cars. Two officers approached the house, their guns drawn. One knocked on the door and they both stood well to the side. I could almost feel their sighs of relief when the door was opened by a young woman with a couple of toddlers, who were excitedly pointing to the police cars. She let them inside the house and, after a quick look around and a few questions, the police returned to their car. We watched as they drove past us, the policeman in the passenger seat of the first car chatting to someone on a radio, presumably to someone in the helicopter.

Emma turned around once the police cars had passed and, once again, we followed at a discreet distance behind them. I had thought the police would have stopped to talk to us, but they must have been given another lead, because they were already hurtling down the track back to the road.

We followed them for about ten kilometres, Emma definitely over the speed limit now, as she endeavoured to keep them in sight. If we lost them, we wouldn't know where they had turned off. I was glad she was driving and not me, as I'm not sure I would have driven more than twenty kilometres over the speed limit.

The next track the police took was off to the right and was very rough. It obviously wasn't used very often, nor maintained. The recent rains had left ruts and several mounds of leaves and small branches littered it. We followed the police for another couple of kilometres before they arrived at what was little more than a hut. There were no vehicles outside and it looked deserted. Again, we watched as the police knocked loudly on the door. When there was no answer, they called out. When no-one replied, the shorter, stockier of the two, shouldered the door and it flew open, whilst his partner pointed his gun at the opening. He came out a couple of minutes later and we heard him call out to the other car that the hut was empty and didn't look as if it had been occupied for some time. We had pulled into a side track and one of the police cars stopped and came over to us.

"What do you think you are doing?" he asked tersely. He was tall and slim, with expressive brown eyes and a young face.

"I'm Emma Watson and it's my husband's killer you're looking for."

"And I'm a friend of David Pearson. I'm hoping you are going to find him today."

"Well, you can't follow us around. Things could get dangerous if we find the right house. You'll have to stop this."

"We won't get in the way and we won't get too close," Emma assured him.

"You still can't be here. Please, when we get back to the road, go back to the roadhouse. I'm sure we have your details on file and we'll contact you as soon as we know anything."

Emma nodded her head, but I knew her well enough by now to know that she had no intention whatsoever of doing as he suggested.

When we got back to the road, she paused for a while

to let the police cars pull ahead. Then she turned to follow them.

"Third time lucky, you reckon?" I asked her.

"Maybe."

Emma stayed well behind the police cars this time. Fortunately, the helicopter above us gave us some indication of where the police cars were. No doubt the police had forgotten all about us, believing their warning would have been sufficient to deter us. They drove for about forty kilometres before turning off. The track would have been easy to miss and we were lucky to see the police turn, as their car quickly disappeared from view, behind a clump of trees. Emma turned on to the track and jammed on the brakes: one of the police cars was parked across the track. They were obviously waiting for us. The same young policeman opened the passenger's door and walked towards us, putting his hat on as he walked.

"I thought I told you ladies, quite clearly, not to follow us. Now, I'm not going to say this again. I do understand that you are as anxious to find Mr Pearson as we are, but you need to stop following us around. Otherwise, I'm going to charge you with hampering a police investigation. Do I make myself clear, this time?"

"Crystal clear, officer," I replied. "Our apologies. We'll leave now and, this time, you have my word that we won't follow you again."

He watched as Emma turned our vehicle around and drove back on to the road, Emma swearing profusely as she drove.

"We did push our luck a bit, Emma."

"But we're here! So close to their investigation! Why can't we be there when they arrest that murderer."

"I think they have a duty of care to the public. They also don't want to be worrying about protecting us if things get nasty. They do have a point, actually."

Chapter Twenty-Two
Moving On

Gary was in a foul mood when Harry and David returned. His foot was badly swollen and very painful. Harry handed him two of the antibiotic tablets and a glass of water, which he swallowed quickly.

"They'd better do the trick, this time," he grumbled as he handed Harry the empty glass.

"You need to see a doctor, I told you that in the first place," Harry replied.

"You know I can't."

"Well, these are much stronger —I think they will work."

David's ankle was throbbing too, but he knew it had been worth aggravating it to get a message to Sandra. She had sounded very happy and relieved to hear his voice. So, they all thought he was dead, too. Well, that made sense after finding Jayden's body and then his disappearance. He hoped it wouldn't be too long before the police found him. He found himself smiling from time to time, imagining the reunion with his family, but he quickly readjusted his face so as not to cause suspicion. He'd have to make sure he didn't get caught in any gunfire. He strained to hear the sound of an approaching vehicle but there was no sound, except for the birds.

Next morning, he was up early, drinking his first cup of coffee for the day. Harry had already finished his and Gary was still asleep. Harry took his phone out of his back pocket and it was then that David realised he hadn't deleted his phone call to Sandra! How could he have been so stupid? Well, he hadn't had much time, but if Harry looked at his call list..... He would have to try and get hold of the phone during the day and delete his call. He could only hope that Harry would put the phone down on the table after he had looked at it and not back in his pocket. Why was he looking at it, anyway? There was no reception here. Boredom, he supposed. David tensed, as Harry continued to play with it. He froze when Harry sat up and looked straight at him. He knew.

"There's an outgoing phone call here that wasn't made by me," he stated. "It was made about the time I left you to get the antibiotics. I think it must have been made by you, David."

David eyes met Harry's glaring stare.

"Who did you ring?" Harry bellowed. "Shall I press redial and see what happens?"

"My, my wife. I rang my wife." David stammered.

"What did you tell her?" Harry shouted.

"I told her I was alive! I told her I'd been kidnapped."

Harry jumped to his feet. David thought he was going to hit him, but he went to find Gary.

"Wake up! Wake up, Gary. David here has alerted the authorities. You have to get out of here. NOW!"

"What?" Gary questioned, still half asleep. He staggered out into the kitchen, bleary-eyed. "What have you done, David?"

"I rang my wife. She was worried sick. I told her I'd been kidnapped. The police will be looking for me by now."

"Where did you tell them you are?" Harry demanded.

"Somewhere near Belyando Crossing. That's all I knew."

"I should have blown your head off weeks ago." Gary stated. "I would have done too, if it wasn't for my foot."

"You have to leave, both of you," Harry declared. "Right now. I can't be caught up in this, whatever it is you've done, Gary. I'll deny knowing you kidnapped David, say I thought he was a friend of yours. You got that, Gary? I didn't know anything, I was only doing a mate a favour."

"Yes, sure. Whatever. How are we going to leave, Harry? Neither of us can drive," Gary wheedled.

"I don't care how you do it. One of you will have to drive - I want you out of here now!"

"Okay, okay, I hear what you're saying. Give me five minutes to get myself sorted. You'll have to drive, David. If you can't manage it, I might as well drop you right here."

"Not on my property, you don't!" Harry bellowed.

"Okay, keep your hair on. We'll be on our way in a jiffy."

"I can drive," David was quick to assure him.

"I'll get you some water to take with you," Harry offered. "Give me your water cans."

Gary hobbled out to his vehicle and Harry followed him. He took two jerry cans and filled them both with water and put them in the back. He made a couple of thick sandwiches too and placed them on the front seat.

Ten minutes later David and Gary were driving down the track to the main road.

Didn't even get a thank-you, Harry thought to himself, as he watched them drive away. *Now I have to wait for the police to call.*

Later that day, Harry watched as two police cars

made their way down the track towards the house. He braced himself and waited as they positioned themselves around the house, guns drawn. On the first knock he opened the door, fashioning a surprised look on his face.

"What can I do for you fellows?" he asked.

"Anyone else in the house?" the young policeman demanded.

"No, I live here alone."

"Step aside, sir and let us come in and check."

Harry stood back and two policemen disappeared inside, their guns drawn, keeping their backs close to the wall. Another policeman stood with his gun trained on Harry and the fourth remained in the police car.

"All clear," the young policeman announced as they came out of the front door.

"What's your name, sir?" his colleague inquired.

"Harry. Harry Duggan."

"Do you have a Driver's Licence, Harry?"

"Yes, I'll go and get it for you."

The policeman's gun followed him as he went inside for his wallet and pulled out his licence. One of the policemen looked at it and nodded to his colleague.

"We're looking for a man whose been kidnapped. David Pearson. We don't know if he was kidnapped by one person or more than one. Can you shed any light on that for us, sir?"

"Er, no. I don't know anything about a kidnap."

The policeman looked around. There was definitely no sign of anyone else in the house.

"There are fresh tyre marks under the tree next to the house. Looks like someone's been here recently."

"Ah yes, a friend of mine called in briefly this morning."

"What was the name of this friend, Harry?"

Harry thought quickly. Should he tell them it was Gary or make up a name? He decided to improvise.

"Barry. He dropped in some milk and bread for me. He's good like that."

"What's Barry's surname?"

"Brown. Barry Brown."

"Would you, by any chance, have been a doctor, Harry?"

Harry cleared his throat. "Yes, officer, I was at one time."

"Disbarred for performing illegal abortions?"

"Yes, but I was only helping those women. They were grateful to me."

"You spent some time in jail, Harry, didn't you?"

"Yes and I don't want to go back there."

"You should co-operate with us, then. This Barry, did he have anyone else in the car with him?"

"No, he was on his own. I told you, I don't know anything about a kidnapping."

"Which direction was Barry heading from here?"

"I didn't ask him, officer. I thanked him for dropping off the bread and milk and he went on his way."

"This kidnapped fellow, David Pearson, he said he and his kidnapper were staying with an ex-doctor called Harry. I find it rather strange that you claim not to know anything about them?"

"He must have been mistaken. Or there's another doctor around called Harry. A retired doctor, perhaps?"

"What sort of vehicle does this Barry drive?"

"A beat-up old Ford."

"You don't happen to know what his number plate is, do you Harry?"

"Sorry, officer. I don't."

The policeman's frustration was obvious in his eyes, but he forced a smile.

"Okay, Harry. Well, thank you for your time."

Harry let out a big sigh of relief as the police cars disappeared from view.

"Do you believe him, Greg?" the young policeman asked his superior.

"Not at all. But I don't think he knows where they were heading, so we'd only be wasting time questioning him further."

David was finding driving painful. His ankle throbbed and he hoped it wouldn't start to swell in the plaster casing. When they reached the road, Gary had ordered him to head south.

"Head towards New South Wales," he instructed. "I've had enough of Queensland. Let's get the hell out of here."

David knew that he had a worse problem than his aching ankle. He knew his only chance of survival was to escape before Gary reached another place of refuge. With his foot starting to heal quite well, very soon he would no longer need David around and he had no doubt that it was Gary's intention to kill him. He couldn't be stuck in the middle of nowhere, alone with Gary.

Chapter Twenty-Three
A Plea for Help

Emma and I returned to the caravan park at Belyando Crossing and discussed our next move.

"Following the police around is obviously not an option, Emma. What else can we do?"

"The police have the advantage. They used a helicopter to search for any out-of-the-way places and had access to Council records to check for any isolated houses. That only leaves a hut or similar structure, hidden from the helicopter by trees. What we need now is some local knowledge – someone who might be aware of a place to hide out that isn't generally known."

"You're thinking of a long-time resident or someone who spends a lot of time in the bush?"

"Yep, that's what I'm thinking."

"I guess we'll be making another visit to the Roadhouse then. I suggest we wait until tonight and go there for dinner. With a bit of luck, we'll have heard from the police before then, about their day's activities."

We decided to make good use of the intervening time by catching up on our washing. We knew it wouldn't take

275

long to dry in the heat. I walked around the other caravans, showing people the photo of David and asking if they had seen him. It was disheartening, as one after the other, they shook their heads. Around four o'clock we joined some of the other caravanners for drinks under a large, shady tree. A tall, slim man, who introduced himself as John, asked why we were looking for David. I told them the story and everyone was very sympathetic, promising to keep an eye out for him on their travels. Whilst we were sitting there, Emma took a phone call from Detective Brady. We both moved away from the group and Emma put the phone on loudspeaker, so that I could hear.

"I hear you've been making a bit of a nuisance of yourselves," was his opening line.

"Only for a little while," Emma replied. "The local police soon let us know we weren't welcome."

"Well, I'm ringing to give you an update. They went to another three houses after you left them. One belonged to a retired doctor, name of Harry. We are pretty sure he is the doctor David was referring to, but there was no-one else at the house and he denied David had ever been there. He told the police that the other tyre marks belonged to a friend who had dropped off some supplies that morning. They didn't believe him; they thought the tyre tracks might have come from the kidnapper's vehicle. However, they were pretty sure that Harry didn't know where they were going, so they let it drop. Hell, they probably didn't know where they were going themselves, if they left in a hurry. We don't know what tipped them off to make the move; we think we only missed them by a couple of hours."

Emma swore.

"The only thing that would have made them leave in a hurry was if the kidnapper somehow found out that David had made the phone call to Sandra," I suggested.

"That's not impossible," Detective Brady responded. "He might not have had a chance to wipe the phone call. Or the kidnapper might have already planned to meet up with someone else, or he could have argued with Harry – out-stayed his welcome."

"Yes, they are all possibilities," I agreed. "Do you have any idea where to look now?"

"Unfortunately, Mrs Davies, we don't."

"Please call me Anna, Detective."

"Okay, Anna. They could be heading in any direction. Not knowing who the kidnapper is, means that we have no idea of his habits or where he might go. We are getting someone from forensics out to this Harry's house to see if the tyre tracks found there match the vehicle that was at the scene of the murder. Harry said they were made by an old Ford, but we'll see."

"That's a good idea. At least then we'll know for sure then that David was there."

"I'll let you know as soon as I hear anything. At the moment, all we can hope for is that someone will see them and recognise David. You put out a lot of posters in the area, I believe. His photo has also been in the papers and on the television. Perhaps someone out there will recognise him and we can get a fix on where they are."

"Or perhaps they will be stopped for a traffic infringement and an eagle-eyed policeman will recognise David," I said. "Isn't that how many criminals are caught?"

"Surprisingly, Anna, yes. A great number of criminals are pulled up for speeding, or other misdemeanour on the road and are recognised and arrested. We are making sure that details of the kidnapping, along with David's photo, are being made available throughout the State."

"They might leave Queensland, if things get too hot,"

Emma said.

"We've circulated the details in New South Wales as well, particularly around the border area."

"You do realise that David's life is in danger?" I asked.

"We are well aware of the danger to his life, Anna. We are doing everything we can and will continue to do so."

"Thank you, Detective."

"I had checks carried out on those HiLux vehicles, by the way. We were able to speak to all of the owners of the vehicles you photographed, so we know that none of them is the kidnapper. It turns out you took a photo of a man we've been looking for over the last few months, for an armed robbery! One of our detectives recognised him from the photo and, having an idea of the area he was in, we have been able to apprehend him. So, your hair-brained idea wasn't quite so useless after all."

"That's good to know!" I responded, taking it as a compliment. "Which photo was it that caught him?"

"The one you took at Springsure."

"The guy who looked like he was on drugs?"

"Yes, that one. He is a known drug offender and it was his drug habit that led to him rob a petrol station, near Rockhampton. He had a gun and frightened the teenage boy behind the counter when he fired a shot, which fortunately went into the ceiling and not the boy. He probably had the shakes and fired it off by mistake. Anyway, he was caught on camera and was easy to identify as he hadn't even bothered to cover his face."

"It's a pity it wasn't David's kidnapper, but I suppose it's better than nothing."

"It did help our clear-up rate!" Detective Brady responded with a chuckle. "So, where are you two going now? Are you heading back to Sydney?"

"We haven't talked about it yet," Emma answered him.

"Well, that would be my suggestion. Go home and leave us to follow up on this. I'm sure we'll find them soon."

"This is impossible!" Emma exclaimed as we poured over the map the next morning. "What do you think, Anna? Which way do you reckon they are heading?"

"Your guess is as good as mine, Emma. If it were me and I didn't want to be found, I'd go north or maybe even further west."

"I suppose that makes sense. How much more driving around aimlessly can we do?"

"I don't know."

Emma sighed. "I think we're kidding ourselves to think we are going to find them. If the police can't locate them, with all their resources, what chance do we have?"

"Are we admitting defeat?"

"I think we have to. I don't like it, but we are getting nowhere. Let's head for home, Anna."

Much as I hated to agree, it did make sense. I thought of Mike and my own bed. We packed up the vehicle and headed south. I wasn't happy to be going home without finding David. I felt I was letting Sandra down.

David decided that his best option might be to try to attract the attention of a police car, by driving erratically. He wasn't sure how much he would be able to get away with before Gary realised what he was trying to do. If they were pulled over, even if the policeman didn't recognise him, he would not be impressed by the fact David was driving with his foot in plaster, which might lead to some sort of questioning. He decided that, if he was lucky enough to spot a police car, some erratic driving might be his best chance.

"We'll need petrol soon," David said a little while later, noting the fuel gauge registering towards empty.

"Yeah, Harry could at least have filled one of our jerry

cans," Gary replied. "You'd better fill up at Emerald."

David knew he didn't have enough cash left to pay for the petrol, so he would have to use his credit card, since Gary never seemed to have any money. That would leave a paper trail. It would tell the police they were heading south. At last, things seemed to be going in his favour. They pulled into a garage on the north side of Emerald and, to his surprise, Gary pulled a handful of dollars from his pocket.

"At least I got something out of Harry. It's amazing what someone will give you when they want to get rid of you!"

David struggled hard to hide his disappointment.

"Fill up those two spare jerry cans too. And get something to eat, whilst you're there. The less we have to stop, the better."

There were two or three cars filling up at the garage. Gary moved his rifle from between his legs and put his hand on the trigger, as a car pulled in on the other side of the fuel pump. There were two young girls in the back.

"See that young girl," he said, pointing at the one closest to them. "Any funny business from you and I'll shoot her."

David was sure he meant it, although he wasn't sure how Gary was going to get away. Perhaps he planned to shoot him as well, before hijacking another car and driver.

Frustrated, David hobbled around to the back of the vehicle and began pumping petrol. When the tank was full, he filled the two jerry cans. As he put the cap back on the last one, he looked up and met Gary's stony glare. He tapped the rifle he was holding, as a reminder of what he would do if David made any attempt to escape. David made his way to the cashier, stopping in the shop to grab bread, tinned ham and tinned soup. As he approached the cashier, he came face to face with himself. There was a poster of him and Jayden stuck on the glass in front of him. He must have gasped, because the man next to him, who was buying coffee, looked at him and then at the poster.

"That could almost be you. Without the beard, like," he commented.

David turned to look at him. He was middle-aged, with a friendly smile and curly light-brown hair.

"It is me," David whispered. "I'm David Pearson. But there's a man out there with a rifle trained on those little girls in the car next to me, so don't say a word. One mistake and he'll shoot them. Trust me."

The man paled. "They're my little girls," he said quietly.

"Well, here's what you do. Go back to your car, get in and drive away. Don't look at him, whatever you do. Pay for your petrol and stuff and then leave. Act normal. When you get down the road, ring the police and tell them you've seen me. I'll write down the registration number of the vehicle, here," David said, grabbing a pamphlet from the counter. "Tell them that's the vehicle I'm in, we're heading south and he has a rifle. You got that?"

The man nodded, his frightened eyes meeting David's briefly.

"Whatever you do, don't look at him. And thank you."

The father of the two girls tucked the pamphlet with the registration number in his shirt pocket, picked up his coffee and ice-creams and quickly returned to his car.

"Receipt?" the cashier asked as he handed him back his change. David declined. He couldn't help but wonder if the father of the girls would ring the police, or would he decide that he didn't want to be involved and keep driving? David knew he had to make the most of this opportunity; there might not be another one. Taking the receipt from the cashier's hand, he wrote down Gary's registration number and handed it back to the young cashier.

"I'm David Pearson," he informed him, nodding towards the poster. "Don't say anything, just listen. The man I'm with has a rifle and he won't hesitate to use it. He's got it trained on a little girl, so don't do anything to arouse his suspicion. Once we've left, please ring the police, tell them I was here and that this is the registration number of the vehicle I'm in. We're heading south. Can you do that for me?"

The dumbfounded cashier nodded his head, looking from David to the poster and back again. He was only in his early, twenties, David thought. Would he be able to help him?

"I'm counting on you," David said as he turned to leave. "This man has a rifle and he is going to kill me."

Nervously, David returned to the vehicle, put the food in the back and slid into the driver's seat.

"We'll stay on this road; cross the border at Goondiwindi," Gary informed him, sliding the rifle down between his legs.

"Where are we heading?" David asked, conversationally.

"I'll let you know when we get there."

David tried not to look in the rear-view mirror too often. He glanced in the side mirrors from time to time, desperately wanting to see a police car coming up behind him. Would either of the men from the petrol station have called the police? Would the police have believed them? How long would it take before they came and rescued him? He hoped it would be before they crossed the border into New South Wales. He wasn't sure if the Queensland police would follow him into New South Wales, or whether the police in that State would take this seriously. *It won't be long now, Sandra*, he promised, assuring himself as much as his wife. *The police will come soon and then I'll be home with you and the girls.*

They were approaching Injune when Gary ordered him off the road.

"We'll camp here overnight," he said. "I don't know what's hurting most, my foot or my knee."

You should try driving with a broken ankle, David thought to himself. His ankle had been throbbing for hours and he felt sure it was swelling. Perhaps if he put it up for a few hours it would settle down. They unfolded a couple of chairs and set them up under a tree, resting their injured legs on the small table between them. David thought Gary looked tired. *Maybe he'll fall asleep in a minute and I can drive away and leave him.*

Gary must have read his mind.

"Better give me the keys. Don't want you going off and leaving me, do we?"

Reluctantly, David handed him the keys and watched Gary push them deep into his shorts' pocket. He knew he couldn't walk far with his broken ankle. They were a couple of kilometres off the main road and he thought about the rifle. If Gary woke after an hour, or less, he would manage to drive and hunt him down. He couldn't see himself escaping tonight.

After a couple of hours' rest, David made them a meal of tinned meat and bread. They both missed Harry's cooking, but they were sufficiently hungry to clean their plates. As darkness fell, Gary produced the handcuffs and cuffed David's right hand to the steering wheel.

"You can put your legs across the passenger seat. I'll sleep in the back. We'll make an early start in the morning," he informed David.

It was not a comfortable night for David. His ankle didn't stop throbbing and trying to sleep, handcuffed to the steering wheel, was not easy. He was glad when Gary stirred soon after five o'clock. At least he had slept well, judging by his snores.

"You look a bit rough, mate," Gary pronounced. "I think my foot is probably better than your ankle now. Probably won't be needing you around much longer!" He gave a sly wink and David knew he was trying to unsettle him. He had succeeded.

Breakfast was a cup of coffee and dry bread, before David folded up the chairs and table and they drove back to the main road. The next sign he saw showed that the border at Goondiwindi was a little under five hundred kilometres – around five hours driving. If the police were looking for them, surely that would be enough time to be found? If Gary's foot had improved, he didn't want to spend another night with him, in case it was his last.

As they drove through Roma, a few kilometres down the road, David jerked upright as he caught sight of a police car in his rear vision. *This must be it! Thank goodness.* Unfortunately, Gary had noticed him tense.

"What's up?" he demanded, trying to look in the side mirror.

"A police car," David responded, cursing himself for giving Gary cause to ask. "I don't want them stopping us and finding out I'm driving with a broken ankle."

Gary's head whipped round, as he scanned the road behind them.

"It's okay, he's turned off now." David tried to keep the disappointment out of his voice as he watched the police car turn down a side street. They hadn't been noticed.

"Well, don't you forget about this rifle. If we do get stopped, you'd better do some fast talking, or I'll take you both out."

"You must have done something pretty bad in the past, if you'd consider shooting a cop. They won't stop looking for you until they find you, if you shoot one of theirs. Especially out here, where community is everything."

Gary looked as if he was going to say something, but changed his mind. He stared moodily out of the side window.

"Don't say I didn't warn you. That's all."

David could only hope that there would be more than one police car involved when, or if, they were stopped and that they were aware that Gary had a rifle and was prepared to use it. He'd have to make sure that he was out of range!

A few minutes later, Gary asked David if he'd given

his wife the registration number of the vehicle

"No, mate. I didn't have time. I only told her I was alive and that I thought I was being held somewhere near Belyando Crossing. Then I saw Harry coming back and I had to hang up."

"Good. Well, that's alright then."

Emma and I pulled into Emerald for the night. It was great to see that our posters were still up in several places around town. We went to the pub for dinner and were tucking into roast lamb and all the trimmings when I saw Barry, from the radio station, coming towards me.

"Hello, girls."

"Hi, Barry. How you doing?" Emma responded.

"Great result, huh?"

"What was?" Emma asked.

"Haven't you heard? It's all over town. That guy you were looking for? He went in to buy petrol. Told young Tom in there that he was the one in the poster. Said that the other guy had a gun and not to do anything until they had left and then to ring the police."

"You're kidding. When was this?" Emma asked.

"This morning. They drove in to get petrol this morning. David, the one's that missing, he saw his photo in there and pointed to it, told them he was David Pearson."

Emma and I looked at each other in disbelief.

"Look, I'll leave you to finish your meal. Good work on the posters."

My phone rang then and it was Detective Brady, to give me the news. He'd been tied up with another case and this was his first chance to call.

"We've alerted all police, especially the patrol cars. They are on the lookout for them. Now that we have the number plate, I'm sure it won't be long before we catch up with them."

We ordered another drink each to celebrate. Before I had a chance to ring Sandra, she called me. Detective Brady had already rung her and she was excited and frightened at the same time.

"I do hope the police can find them soon, Anna. I can't wait for David to be rescued and come home."

"It shouldn't be long now," I assured her. "You won't believe this, but we are actually in Emerald right now!"

"You are? How cool is that? You must have been right behind him, Anna!"

"I know." I decided not to mention that we were actually on our way back to Sydney. There were some things even best friends didn't need to know.

"I'm worried he might get hurt when the police pull the car over. I couldn't bear it if something was to happen to him now."

"The police know their job, Sandra. You have to trust them to rescue David safely."

"I know, but this waiting is killing me."

I hung up from Sandra and rang Mike. He hadn't heard the news but was relieved to think the saga was drawing to a close.

"You'll be able to come home now, Anna."

"Yes, I didn't tell Sandra, but we're already heading that way. Would you believe we are at Emerald?"

"In that case, I'll see you soon, darling."

Goondawindi was not far away now. Roma was quite a big town and David's hopes had been pinned on being spotted as they drove through. Now he had to hope that a roving police car would see them. He wondered if there would be anyone monitoring the border at Goondawindi, but he doubted it. Soon they would be in New South Wales, closer to home, but probably more unlikely to be spotted. He figured Gary was planning to kill him, once they were in

New South Wales, sometime over the next day or two. He couldn't let that happen, not when he was so close to Sandra. He'd survived this long, he had to make it home to his girls.

Chapter Twenty-Four
The Nightmare Ends

An hour-and-a-half later, David noticed a police car coming towards them. Maybe this time! It was a straight stretch of road, giving him no chance to commit a traffic offence, unless he started weaving across the centre line. Gary would realise straight away what he was doing. Was it worth trying?

"No funny business," Gary warned. He had seen the police car as well.

David peered into the police car as it passed him. He saw the policeman in the passenger seat say something to the driver. Was he saying something about their vehicle? Both he and Gary watched in the mirrors as they passed. David let out a deep breath as he watched the car stop on the side of the road and turn around. It was coming up behind them! Had they recognised the number plates or had they been given another job to attend? He lightly touched the brake lights, flicking them on and off, on and off, so they would know he had seen them. If only there was another police car as back-up.

Gary had seen the police car turn around and swivelled around in his seat to look through the back window.

"They're coming after us!" he screamed. "Get moving; leave them behind."

"No, that will only alert them to a problem. It's probably nothing, just routine. They'll pull us over, we'll answer their questions and they'll go away. I expect they're bored; looking for something to do. They may even go past us, on another job."

"Floor it!"

"No. We can't outrun that V8 anyway."

The police car was beside them by now, the policeman in the passenger seat indicating with his hand that they should pull over. David was aware of the policeman looking intently inside their vehicle. He glanced at him, with what he hoped was a pleading look. Then he put on the left blinker and slowed the car. As he pulled on to the shoulder of the road, the police car pulled in front of them, before backing up to within a couple of inches of theirs, so there was no room to pull around it.

Gary swore. "You'd better handle this, or you'll all be dead."

Both policemen got out of their car, their guns drawn. One stood behind the car, presumably for protection. The driver stood behind his open door.

"Get out of the car, driver!" the senior officer yelled.

"What are they doing? Why are they standing back there?" Gary demanded, wild-eyed.

David didn't comment. Slowly opening the door, he struggled to a standing position. He copied the police driver's actions, leaving the door open, but standing in front of it, for protection from the rifle. If Gary started shooting, he didn't want to be hit. What would Gary do now? Would he try to shoot his way out of this?

By this time, the police had their guns trained on Gary.

"Now you, sir," the policeman ordered, pointing at Gary. "Get out of the car."

"He's got a gun!" David yelled, as he ducked down behind the door.

Gary swung open his door and pushed the rifle into the gap between the car and the door.

"Don't do that, sir!" one of the policemen shouted. "We want to ask you some questions, that's all."

Gary realised that, by raising the rifle, he had given himself away. David risked a glance at Gary through the window. Would he surrender or would he start shooting? David had no idea which way this was going to go. Gary might well decide on a shoot-out. If he killed both the policemen, he could order David back into the car and he knew he would be no better off than he was before. That is, if he didn't shoot him here.

"Drop the rifle," the senior policeman shouted, "or we will shoot."

Gary was still trying to decide whether to give himself up or shoot, when another police car pulled in behind them. David's instinct was to stand up; he didn't want the occupants of the new police car to mistake him for a criminal, but common-sense made him stay down in front of the door.

Gary turned at the sound of the police car pulling up behind him. Slowly, he pulled the rifle back inside the car.

"Good decision, sir. Now, throw the rifle out on to the ground – as far away from the car as you can."

David heard the clatter of the rifle as it landed on the ground and sighed with relief. He looked up to see two policemen get out of the car parked behind them and walk towards Gary's side of the car. One picked up the rifle, the other ordered Gary out of the vehicle.

"You're okay now, Mr Pearson," the senior officer from the first police car called out. "You can stand up slowly and walk towards us."

David had never been more pleased in his life. He straightened up and limped over to the police car. At last, the nightmare was over.

The senior policeman moved forward to meet him, holding out his hand. The other policeman still had his gun trained on David.

"David Pearson? Sergeant Kennedy. Very good to meet you, sir."

David shook his hand and the Sergeant put a hand on his shoulder.

"How are you?"

"Good. It's such a relief to see you guys."

His partner holstered his gun.

"How's that ankle?"

"Hurts like hell. I think it's swelling. I wasn't intending to drive with it in plaster."

"No, well, we'll overlook that, this time. I'm afraid you'll have to come to the station with us and answer some questions. We'll need you to make a statement too."

"What's the name of that guy," he asked, indicating Gary with his head.

"I only know him as Gary. I know he killed two people in the Northern Territory – a jeweller and his daughter."

"The car is registered to a Greg Mainsbridge. The address he used took us to a vacant block. He registered it under a false name and address."

David was helped to the back seat of the police car. He saw Gary being put into the other police car. At the police station, Gary was taken to a cell and David to an interview room.

"Right, we need you to tell us everything that happened, right from the beginning. Do you need a doctor to look at your ankle or can it wait until after we do this?"

"It hurts like hell, but I'd rather get this sorted out. First though, can I please ring my wife?"

"Yes, sure. Here, use my phone," Sergeant Kennedy replied, handing him his mobile.

"Sandra? Sandra, it's me, David. I'm safe. The police have rescued me. Yes, yes, I'm fine. They caught up with us between Roma and Goondoowindi. Yes, I'll be home soon. I can't wait to see you and the girls. I'd love to speak to them, but I guess they are at school? Okay, not to worry. I'll ring you again soon when I know when I'll be home. I might need to stop off at a hospital and have this plaster taken off my ankle first; it's swelling like mad. Yes, love you too. Bye for now. See you soon."

David handed the Sergeant his phone. It took David nearly an hour to tell the police what had happened to him. In the meantime, Gary had been fingerprinted and his identity confirmed: Gary Fraser, thirty-three years old, wanted for two murders in the Northern Territory. There was a warrant out for his arrest. The car they were driving wasn't stolen; Gary had bought it, but registered it under a false name and address. It didn't take the police long to confirm that they believed David when he said he hadn't killed Jayden. His statement was printed out and brought to him for signature.

"Which hospital do you want to go to, David? There's one at Roma and one at St George."

"St George, please. I want to keep heading south, towards home!"

Sergeant Ron Kennedy and Constable John Durham pulled up outside the St George Hospital. Constable Durham went inside to arrange for a nurse to bring a wheelchair and David was wheeled inside for an x-ray to check on the damage to his ankle. Unfortunately, the x-ray machine wasn't working and they were waiting on a technician to arrive to fix it. Sergeant Kennedy bought David a coffee and a salad roll from the café inside the hospital. A nurse gave him some painkillers and he was soon feeling more comfortable. The nurse told him they would wait for half-an-hour for the technician and if the machines wasn't working by then, they would take the plaster off anyway.

In the meantime, Detective Brady had been advised of the capture of Gary Fraser and the successful rescue of his hostage. He wasted no time in putting in a call to Sandra, but she had already spoken to David and knew he was safe. His next call was to Emma.

"They've got them!" he announced. "Picked them up about an hour ago, between Roma and St George. David is fine. His ankle is giving him problems so they're taking him to St George Hospital for an x-ray. His kidnapper, Gary Fraser, is on his way to the police station in Brisbane. He's wanted for a number of offences."

Emma punched the air. "They've got them, Anna!

They've got Jayden's killer. David's fine too," she added.

I stopped on the side of the road, whilst we finished talking to Detective Brady and Emma switched her phone to speaker so that I could listen.

"A local police car passed them and the young constable recognised the black HiLux and the number plates. They turned around and pulled them over. It looked like Gary was going to shoot at them for a while, but they had called it in and fortunately another police car was in the vicinity. It drove up behind Gary's vehicle and blocked him in. It was all over in a few seconds, with no shooting, no-one injured. David's been driving with his ankle in plaster, so he's gone to St George Hospital for an x-ray to see if it's swollen. Then he'll be on his way home."

"What will happen to Gary Fraser?" Emma demanded to know.

"He's wanted for the murder of two people in the Northern Territory, as well as the murder of your husband. He's being taken to the watch-house at Brisbane. He won't be wandering around committing any more murders."

Emma and I looked at each other. I couldn't help the tears of joy which spilt down my face and Emma looked close to crying herself. It couldn't have been a better outcome.

"Thank goodness for that! I want to see David, Detective," I told him. "Would he still be at the hospital?"

"He's still on his way to St George hospital. Where are you now?"

"We're nearly at Roma."

"Okay. I'll give you the phone number of Sergeant Kennedy. He's with David and you"ll be able to speak to him. David can decide if he wants to wait for you."

"He'd better," I said to Emma after Detective Brady rang off, "after all we've been through!"

Whilst Emma drove, I rang Sergeant Kennedy's phone. I explained who I was and asked if I could speak to David.

"Certainly, Mrs Davies. Just a moment, I'll put him on."

"David? How are you? I'm so glad you're okay."

"Anna? I'm fine. Terrific, even. How did you find me?"

"We've been in Queensland looking for you. It's been like looking for a needle in a haystack, but I'm so glad you're alive and well."

"It's been a nightmare, Anna. I'm so glad to be out of it."

"It's so good to hear your voice. Have you spoken to Sandra yet?"

"Yes, I have. She's pretty stoked!"

"I bet. You have a broken ankle, I believe?"

"Yep, my right foot. I was forced to drive with it and I'm sure it's swelling up inside the plaster. Sergeant Kennedy and Constable Durham are driving me to St George Hospital to have it removed.

"We can be there in about two hours. We're leaving Roma now. Do you want to hang on and we'll drive you home, or what do you want to do?"

"That sounds terrific to me, Anna. I'm sure the police would arrange something for me but I'd much rather travel with you."

"Okay then, we'll come to the hospital as soon as we can."

"He's okay. He wants us to pick him up at St George Hospital," I told Emma, as I hung up.

"That's great. He can tell us all about this mongrel who killed my Jayden."

"Oh, Emma! I'm so sorry. I'm just so happy that David's been found alive and happy for Sandra and the girls too. For a moment, I forgot about Jayden. None of this changes anything for you."

"Yes, it does! I'm as pleased as you are that David is okay and I'm ecstatic that Jayden's killer has been caught. Hopefully, he'll be put away for a long time and won't be able to hurt anyone else. I hated thinking he was still out there somewhere; that someone else might have to go through what I've been through. I needed to know that Jayden's killer was going to be brought to justice."

Chapter Twenty-Five
A Happy Reunion

My reunion with David, at St George Hospital, was quite emotional. He was sitting with his back to me when I arrived, so I walked up behind him and put my hands on his shoulders. He looked up and smiled and I was distressed to see how tired and drawn he looked. He struggled to his feet and wrapped me in an embrace.

"It is so good to see you, David!" I exclaimed.

"You too, Anna. It is such a relief to think it's all over."

He gave Emma a hug and said how truly sorry he was about Jayden. Emma nodded, bravely fighting tears.

"He was a good man, Emma. He took good care of me on our camping trip. I learned a lot. He didn't deserve to die like that."

"Thank you, David. I miss him so much. The police told me he wouldn't have known much about it."

"No, nothing. One minute he was reaching for the wheel brace, the next he was dead – as quick as that."

"I'm glad. Anyway, we're here to take you home, David," she said simply.

"Well, I'm ready to go. As you can see," he replied,

pointing to his ankle, "as I suspected, the ankle had swollen, so they took the plaster off and bandaged it. I had to promise to go to a hospital when I'm home, to have it re-plastered."

"Sorry you had to wait for us."

"It wasn't long actually. The x-ray machine was broken and they didn't want to take the plaster off without an x-ray. We had to wait for the technician to arrive."

David shook hands with Sergeant Kennedy and thanked him for taking him to the hospital and staying with him. He sank into the wheelchair which a nurse had provided and I pushed him out to the car.

"You sit in the back, David. You'll have more room for your ankle," I suggested.

Emma found a couple of pillows and we propped him up on the back seat. Emma took the wheel and we left the hospital car-park, heading for home. I was nearly as excited at the thought of my own bed and Mike, as I was at seeing my friend's face when I delivered her husband home.

David rang Sandra on my phone straight away and they had a long, animated conversation. Then I rang

Mike to bring him up to date, telling him to expect me home in the early hours of the morning.

"I'm guessing you don't want to overnight anywhere?" I had inquired of David.

"You're right about that! All I want is to see Sandra and my girls."

"It's about a ten-hour drive from here, but with both of us driving, we can go straight through," Emma stated.

"You should try and get some sleep," I suggested to David.

"I probably will, but at the moment I'm too hyped up. Tell me how you came to be looking for me."

I told David how Sandra had been frantic with worry when he hadn't returned from the camping trip and she hadn't heard from him and how she had begged me to try to find him. She knew she had to stay at home with the girls; to be there in case he returned. I told him how Emma had borrowed a camper and how we had driven around, somewhat aimlessly. We had talked to people in pubs, restaurants, petrol stations, everywhere. We had also spoken with tourists, business owners and, by pure luck, the radio station at Emerald. The radio station had been very helpful and put out a call about you and Jayden several times. Naturally we had put up posters wherever we went, but we had absolutely no idea where you were. We just knew that something was wrong. The police had checked your credit cards and phones and knew that you had travelled as far as Dingo, but after that the trail went cold. Emma thought Jayden might have headed for Cooktown, a favourite drive of his. We were going to head up that way, but decided to visit Longreach and Winton first, to see if you had mentioned to anyone where you were heading next, even though the police had scoured the area.

Then we got the news that Jayden was dead and you were missing. When we learned that Jayden had been found in Blackdown Tableland Park, Emma had insisted on driving to the spot where he died. The police had searched the area with dogs for any trace of you, David. When the dogs couldn't find a trail more than a few feet around the vehicle, they determined that you must have been kidnapped by the killer. Or that you were the killer! Can you imagine? I told them in no uncertain terms that there was no way you would have shot Jayden!"

"Yes, the police told me they had thought I could have been the killer," he said with a laugh. "Once they rescued me and learned Gary's identity though, they soon believed me."

"We told them it wouldn't have made sense for you to kill Jayden and not take the vehicle. Where were you going to go on foot?" Emma said.

"We then drove to Rockhampton, where Jayden's body and his vehicle had been taken. Emma had to identify his clothing and tattoo," I continued, glancing at Emma. "The forensic people thought Jayden had been lying in the bush for two or three weeks and his body, well, with decomposition and animals, it wasn't possible to identify him facially. Fortunately he had a tattoo on his wrist – Peter – the name of his son, who died."

"Oh, yes, I remember asking him about the tattoo," David interjected.

"They had already found his driver's licence and were almost certain it was Jayden's body. They checked his dental records too."

I saw Emma tense as she remembered that day.

"They found your mobile phone in the vehicle," I added.

"I knew they would. I was so annoyed I hadn't managed to grab it. Still, there wasn't any mobile phone coverage in the places I was held. How was Jayden found?"

"A couple of tourists saw the vehicle parked in the

bush and were curious. Most people would have driven past, but they decided to stop and have a look around. Maybe they were hoping to steal something out of it, who knows? Probably not though, as the vehicle was unlocked and they didn't take your phone. They found Jayden behind the slide-on camper. They were pretty shaken up, as you would expect."

"After Jayden's funeral," Emma continued, "we came back to Rockhampton and picked up the camper and started searching for you again. When the police arranged for a helicopter to fly over the area of Belyando Crossing, looking for the isolated house where you were being held, we tried to follow the police car. We were soon told, in no uncertain terms, to leave it to them! We were asking around in Emerald again when someone said you had been seen in the petrol station and had asked for help. Not long after that, we were told you had been rescued and were safe."

"Thank goodness you put those posters up everywhere! It made it so easy for me to be able to identify myself and get help quickly. I didn't have time for big explanations with Gary waiting, rifle at the ready."

"It was such a relief, David, to know you were safe.

Sandra has been so worried and was beginning to lose faith that you would be found alive. She must be so excited!"

At the sound of Sandra's name, David jerked and opened his eyes. I hadn't noticed that he had started to fall asleep.

"You must be exhausted, David. Try to sleep. You can tell us what happened to you when you wake up."

It wasn't long before David was snoring. I closed my eyes and tried to rest. It would be my turn to drive soon. The tension of the last few hours caught up with me and I closed my eyes and let myself drift.

I woke as the vehicle came to a stop at a petrol pump. Checking my watch, I could see I had been asleep for a couple of hours. I opened the car door and stepped out and stretched. After paying for the fuel, I swapped places with Emma. David didn't stir.

After driving for three hours, I pulled into another petrol station. Emma had been asleep for most of the time I was driving. We didn't need petrol but we did need a toilet break and coffee. Taking it in turns to visit the restrooms, so as not to leave David alone, I returned with three cups of coffee.

"Hmm, coffee. That smells good," David said, opening his eyes and stretching.

"How's the ankle?" I asked, as he took one of the paper cups from me.

"Still throbbing. It's okay though."

"Do you want something to eat?"

"Yes please, I'm starving."

I parked the car outside a Hungry Jack's and we went inside to order. We ate our burgers in the café.

"I suppose it's too late to ring my girls now?" David asked, as we finished eating.

"No way!" I exclaimed. "They'll be happy to be woken up to hear from their dad."

David borrowed my phone and rang the number.

"Hi, darling. Is it too late to speak to Avril and Bethany? We've stopped at a Hungry Jack's and there's good reception here."

He waited whilst Sandra woke the girls and then we put the phone on to speaker so that he could speak to them both at once. Bethany shrieked when she heard her father's voice and Avril was laughing. It was a very happy conversation, with David promising to see them soon.

When he finished talking to them, we returned to the

vehicle and were soon back on the road again, with Emma driving. It was already past ten o'clock and there wasn't much traffic on the road.

"So, David, do you think you can give us a quick rundown on what happened to you and Jayden?" I asked.

"Yes, of course. I think I owe it to you! We were already heading for home. Jayden mentioned there was some Aboriginal art in the Blackdown National Park, not far from where we were. I had never seen any Aboriginal drawings so I was keen to see them. We walked along the cultural trail and found the handprints. I wasn't very impressed actually, they weren't much to look at but still, I was pleased I had seen them. Afterwards we decided we might as well drive the loop road, but half-way round we blew a back tyre. Jayden reversed into the bush to change it, as it was quite a narrow track. Whilst he was changing it, another vehicle stopped on the road in front of us. The guy got out and asked us if we needed a hand. Jayden thanked him and told him he was just tightening the nuts on the spare tyre. He seemed friendly, asked us where we had been and stayed chatting. We told him we were on our way home, having been as far as Barcaldine and that we'd spent some time fossicking for gems around Emerald. He asked if we had found anything and we told him we found a few smaller ones, but hadn't had much luck. He told us his name was Gary and that he was cruising around and then he returned to his vehicle. Jayden was wheeling the flat tyre to the back of the slide-on camper when he looked over my shoulder. Gary had returned, holding a rifle, and demanded we hand over the gemstones. There was no-one else around, so we had no choice. There was nothing of much value. The best was a sapphire I found, which I was going to have made into a ring for Sandra, but it wasn't very big."

David sighed. "For some reason, as I passed the gemstones to Gary, Jayden saw the wheel brace and decided he was going to have a go. I think he was worried that he might shoot us anyway. I'd wondered the same thing myself. It was his eyes, you know? They were sort of glazed over and cold-looking. But Gary saw him reach for the wheel brace and shot him, bang, straight through the forehead."

David paused and turned to look at Emma.

"I'm sorry, Emma. It must be hard for you to hear this."

"I need to know what happened," Emma replied, her hands gripping the wheel tightly.

"Do you want me to drive, Emma? I asked.

"No, it's okay. I'm fine."

"Jayden didn't know anything, Emma," David assured her. "He was dead before he hit the ground. Gary let me check his pulse and there was no doubt about it. The mongrel just left him there; forced me into his vehicle," David said, his voice full of emotion. "Not before I managed to do some damage to him though. After he shot Jayden, I think he was a bit shocked. He put the rifle down and stood it against the vehicle. I don't think he had meant to shoot him, it was like a reflex action. One minute Jayden was alive and changing the tyre, the next he was lying on the ground, dead. He bent down to check Jayden's pulse himself. Then he searched his pockets, pulling out his wallet and removing the notes. Whilst Gary was distracted transferring the money to his own wallet, I picked up the wheel brace and smashed it down on his foot, twice. Then I took another swing whilst he was still off-guard. I should have gone for his head, but somehow, I couldn't do that. I smashed it across his knee instead. He grabbed the rifle then and pointed it at me. I thought he was going to leave me for dead too and I think he would have done, but I had done some real damage to his foot. He was staring down at it, watching the blood pour out if it. Then he ordered me into the driver's seat and told me to start driving. From there on, I was his prisoner. He handcuffed me to the steering wheel whilst he slept. We went to an old hut he knew about in the bush and stayed there for a few days. It was very basic. His foot wasn't healing though, he needed antibiotics. He decided to go to a friend of his, this de-registered doctor, Harry. He wasn't too pleased to see us but he owed Gary for something, so he took us in. He'd been involved in a robbery that went wrong in the Northern Territory, I learned later. I don't know if he was a willing participant in that or not, but I'm sure the police will find out. Anyway, Harry had contact with another doctor who was still practising and he managed to get some antibiotics. Gary asked to stay there for a couple of days. I could see that Harry wasn't at all keen, but he agreed. Then it started raining and the nearby river flooded and we were stuck there. Gary's foot was improving every day and I knew he wasn't going to let me go. He would have to kill me at some point.

I tried to escape one night but Harry caught up with me and threw me to the ground. I managed to unbalance him – he isn't very fit. Unfortunately, he landed on top of me and he's a big man. My ankle was caught underneath me and something broke. Then he had two invalids on his hands. He wasn't very pleased about that, as you can imagine."

"No, I'm sure he wasn't!" Emma agreed.

"Gary's foot started to swell again, as soon as he finished the course of antibiotics. It was smashed up pretty badly and probably needed an operation or something. I heard them talking one night and learned about the killing of the jeweller and his daughter. There was no way Gary was going to a doctor or hospital. Harry went back to his doctor friend to get some stronger antibiotics. Gary was in a hell of a mood and I asked Harry to take me with him. He had taken me the first time he went for antibiotics. I told him Gary was likely to kill me if he left me behind, he was so angry. Harry was reluctant to take me along, but he did. He handcuffed me to the door handle when he went into the doctor's, but, as luck would have it, on this second trip, his phone fell out of his pocket as he got out of the car. I was able to grab it and ring Sandra. He came back before I could tell her much, but obviously it was enough."

"Yes, the police put a helicopter up, to try and locate

you."

"The next day, Harry discovered I had made a phone call on his mobile. I didn't have time to erase it. He told us to pack up and leave straight away, he didn't want us there any longer. I was driving, trying to decide if I should commit a traffic infringement if I saw a police car, to draw attention to myself, but I was worried Gary might shoot us both. In the end, it was easy. We needed petrol and I stopped at the gas station at Emerald. I couldn't believe it when I saw a photo of myself at the counter! Another customer told me I could be that man, without the beard. I told him it was me, but that the man who had taken me hostage had a gun trained on two little girls in the car next to ours. He went white – it was his car and his girls. I asked him to return to the car as if nothing had happened and, when he got down the road, to ring the police and give them the registration number. Gary had me change the number plates for a spare pair he had with him. I had memorised the number and wrote it down for him, on a flyer. Then I wrote the number down again on the receipt the cashier gave me and gave it back to the cashier when I paid. I pointed to the poster on the glass and told him I was the man on the poster and the man I was with had a gun and wasn't afraid to use it. I asked him to ring the police after I left. He nodded, but I still couldn't be sure he would do it. I thought one of them might ring, maybe both, but I couldn't be sure. I knew I didn't have long before Gary was going to be able to drive himself and would no longer need me around.

As I drove, I was watching the side mirrors for any sign of a police car. Nothing happened that day and we pulled into the bush near Injune overnight. The next day we were getting close to the border and I wasn't sure how interested the New South Wales police would be in stopping us. Then a police car passed us, taking a good look inside our vehicle. I couldn't believe it when it did a U-turn and sped up behind us. Gary told me to floor it, but I said they were probably only doing a casual check; we'd answer their questions and be on our way. No need to attract attention to ourselves and their car was more powerful than ours, anyway. We wouldn't outrun them on a straight road. The police pulled us over and parked right in front of us, so we couldn't go forward. Gary was threatening to kill both the policeman and me. Then another police car pulled up behind us and it was all over. He threw the rifle out of the car, as directed and gave himself up. The relief! It was all so easy in the end. No-one else hurt and I was free!"

"You are going to have quite a tale to tell Sandra and the girls," I commented.

"I can't wait to see them, Anna. How much longer, do you think, before we get there?"

"About three-and-a-half hours, if we continue like this. There's not much traffic, so we are making good time."

"Time for another snooze then!" David replied.

Three hours and forty minutes later we drew up at David's front door. All the lights in the house were on and Sandra flung the front door open the minute she heard the car pull up. Behind her, Bethany and Avril flew down the steps. David struggled to his feet and moved towards them. Sandra fell into his arms, crying and laughing. David pulled her close and hugged her tight. Then he opened his right arm to encircle his girls. We watched for a minute and then Emma backed out of the drive. Sandra looked up over David's shoulder and waved.

"Thank you," she mouthed into the headlights.

Emma and I looked at each other, tears pooling in our own eyes. Then she drove me home to Mike.

Chapter Twenty-Six
The End of an Adventure

Mike was also waiting up and opened the front door to our apartment before I could knock. He must have been listening out for us. I felt awful saying goodbye to Emma, knowing her husband would not be waiting at home for her, but I did know she was looking forward to visiting her mother in the nursing home later in the day.

I was drawn into a pair of loving arms and Mike's kiss told me he was pleased I was home again. After I had showered, we sat up drinking coffee and I told him everything I knew about David's adventure.

"As you said from the beginning, the chances of us finding David were pretty much zilch. Australia is a huge country and we were lucky he didn't make it out of Queensland. I kept looking because it helped Sandra to believe that something was being done, but we didn't have a clue where he was."

"But the posters which you put up everywhere made it so much easier for him to identify himself when he went into that petrol station. One guy recognised him from his picture and he was able to ask for help from both him and the cashier. Plus, it was you and Emma who brought him home. Not only that, but two wanted criminals, Gary and the drug guy who had committed an armed robbery, were caught. Once again, my darling wife, you have helped to solve a mystery."

I smiled. It didn't feel as if we had been able to do much, but somehow it was enough.

"But from now on, I'd like you to stay at home and keep away from danger!"

"I will," I promised happily.

"Did you think about what could have happened if you had stumbled across the pair of them? You could have been shot. I hope you haven't forgotten that, after your adventure in France, you promised me you wouldn't get involved again; not that I would have asked you not to help Sandra. I understood when you said you had to try and do something for her: after all, she is your best friend. But, do you think you are ready to live a normal life now?"

"Definitely. Besides, a promise is a promise."

It was so good to be home. The luxury of a queen-size bed - with Mike in it. The joy of being only a couple of steps from the bathroom with copious hot water, essential oils, moisturisers, hair nourishing cream, not to mention a kitchen I could almost dance in. No more camping for me – ever!

Over dinner that evening, I tried to explain to Mike what it was like in the outback, the endless roads through flat, bush country, the red of the dirt and how it permeated everything, even with the windows closed. I talked about the stars at night when we were free-camping, how there were millions and millions of them once you were away from the lights of the towns. That was probably the best part of our trip. We tend to take stars for granted, we know they are up there, but when there is nothing at all around you and you look up into the inky blackness and see millions of twinkling stars, as far as the eye can see, it is a truly awesome experience. I told him about the kangaroos we saw with babies in their pouches, the koala near the ablutions block at Emerald and the camels. I had to admit to him that they hadn't been wild camels, but it was only bad luck that we hadn't encountered any wild ones, when you think how many there are in Australia. Mike asked about the road-trains and I said how frightening they were as they thundered towards you, commandeering the road.

"And the birds!" I exclaimed. "I didn't expect to see birds in the outback but we saw a lot, especially near water, like the Warrego River or a lake. There was everything from falcons and wedge-tailed eagles to parrots of all colours, Major Mitchell cockatoos, white-necked herons and honeyeaters. Sometimes we'd drive for ages without seeing any birds and then we'd stop somewhere and they would be all around us. It was amazing."

"Well, thanks to your good descriptions, I don't feel as if I need to go and see for myself, so I'm staying well away from the outback," Mike informed me, when I finally ran out of things to relate.

"It's the sheer size of it that you can't comprehend. The vastness and the nothingness."

With some difficulty, I forced myself to leave David and Sandra alone, knowing they would need time to enjoy being together again, with their two girls. Three days later Sandra rang and invited us over for dinner in the evening.

"If you're sure you two lovebirds are ready for visitors!"

"Definitely. Besides, I owe you so much. You brought David back home to me."

"Well, I suppose that's technically correct!"

We arrived with a bottle of champagne and a big box of chocolates. Sandra wrapped her arms around me and squeezed me tight. David kissed me on both cheeks and the girls both thanked me for bringing their daddy home. It was great to see them all so happy and relaxed. Bethany and Avril sat on either side of David on the sofa, snuggling in close.

"They haven't let him out of their sight since he came home," Sandra commented as I went into the kitchen to help her carry the food into the dining room. "They saw him on the television and they seem to realise how lucky we are that he came back to us."

Naturally, David's kidnap and rescue were all over the news for a few days. Journalists had camped outside their house, hoping for a personal interview but, fortunately, they had left that morning, realising that neither David nor Sandra would be making a statement. I was glad we were not forced to push our way through them to reach the front door. Emma had also been in the news, with a passing mention of how she had travelled to Queensland with a friend in an attempt to find out what happened to her husband. David and Jayden's photos had been splashed widely across the media.

"Daddy," Avril said, tapping her father's arm to get his attention. "Did you see any dingoes when you were in the outback?"

"Yes, darling, a few."

"What were they like?"

"They were completely wild. I suppose they look a bit like a cross between a pet dog and a fox. They are very cunning."

"Were they scary?" she asked, her eyes wide.

"Not really. They didn't come very close to us."

"Well, dinner is ready now," Sandra called out from the kitchen. "Let's eat and talk about something else!"

Mike and I took the hint and talked to Avril and Bethany about school and their hobbies, over a salmon salad and trifle. After the girls had gone to bed, we sat in the lounge drinking coffee and liqueurs.

"We had a phone call from Detective Brady this morning,' David informed us. "He confirmed what I had overheard Gary and Harry talking about, you know, the robbery where the jeweller and his daughter were shot. No wonder Gary didn't want to be found!"

"He had killed before, I take it?" Mike asked.

"Yes, he had. As you know, I heard them talking about a robbery gone wrong, and the police confirmed that it happened. They knew that Gary had another man with him but, so far, he hasn't told them his name. The owner of the jewellery shop was an old man and they probably thought it was an easy job, but he surprised them by pulling a gun out from under the counter. They know he fired the gun and Gary then shot him. The jeweller's granddaughter was helping out in the shop and came out from the back room to see what had happened and he shot her too. As they ran out to their car, a bystander took down the number plate. The witness said that neither man appeared to have been wounded. The police knew from the car registration and the description that it was Gary and issued a warrant for his arrest. He hadn't even used a different car! They found it, abandoned in the bush, sometime later. I knew, from listening to Gary talk, that he had been hiding in the bush ever since, which was why they never found him. Detective Brady said they had no idea who the other man was, but I told Detective Brady that it was Harry. Don't forget, Harry was living in a pretty isolated spot too."

"So, they are going to arrest Harry?" I asked.

"Yes, I think they already have. Detective Brady also said I would get the gemstones back. I'll give them to

Emma, I think. I don't need any reminders of this part of my life!"

"I can understand that. I bet Harry is cursing Gary – and you! He'd managed to hide himself away and live a quiet life. Do you think Gary had killed before the Northern Territory murders?" I asked David. "I mean, he didn't have to kill Jayden. He had a rifle pointed at you, but he could have taken the gemstones and disappeared. From what you told us, firing the rifle was almost like an automatic reaction."

"I see what you mean," David replied, his forehead creased in a frown. "I don't know. Detective Brady didn't mention any other murders."

"I've been looking into unsolved murders in Queensland. There were the unsolved murders of that elderly couple found in their house in Central Queensland, near Winton, a few years back and the young man who went missing on an outback adventure somewhere around Concurry three years ago. His body was never found, nor any trace of him. The same thing with the couple who went camping around Mt Isa and disappeared. That's a mystery, if ever I saw one. The police are pretty sure they are all dead. In fact, there have been quite a few unsolved disappearances and murders in the outback over the years."

"I'm sure the police will question him thoroughly, Anna," Mike answered, with an edge to his voice.

I knew he was warning me not to even think about getting involved in any of these unsolved murders. He didn't have to worry, though, I had no intention of returning to the outback.

There's nothing like a mystery to make time fly! We were now approaching the half-way mark in Mike's contract and racing towards Christmas. It would be my first Christmas in a hot climate for many years and I was looking forward to it. I loved the crisp air in London at Christmas-time, the shops filled with decorations and the beautiful window-displays, the lights along Bond and Regent Streets and the ever-present possibility of snow and of making a snowman. People rushed around the shops to buy presents, bundled up in beautiful coats and scarves, trying to keep warm. Carol singers stood and sang on street corners, the hot chestnut vendors stood by their braziers roasting the chestnuts and everyone seemed much happier at Christmas time. An Australian Christmas was very different, occurring in the hottest part of the year. Christmas trees, tinsel and lights seemed out of place, even to me. The shop decorations were sparse, as if they couldn't be bothered to make the effort and carol singers were rare, mainly the Salvation Army. What I did love, was the chance to eat Christmas lunch outside, often cold turkey or seafood, or a picnic at the beach dressed only in a swimsuit.

It was a wonderful surprise when Simon rang to say that he, Kelly and young Thomas were flying out to Sydney to spend Christmas with us. Then he added that James and Andrea were coming too! We were so excited! James and Andrea would be able to stay in the apartment with us, but I needed to find some accommodation for Simon and his family, somewhere that was close by. What a Christmas it would be! It was their first trip to Australia for all of them and I wanted it to be special. I worried about how they would cope with the heat, especially our young grandson, Thomas. I would have to make sure that their apartment had air-conditioning. In the end I decided, if we were going to rent an apartment, it might as well be a big one that would take all of us. I found the perfect place – a huge house at Manly, on the beach, where we could all be together for two weeks.

Christmas Day dawned, with clear blue skies and a light breeze, exactly as I remembered it. We exchanged presents and took our time over a cooked breakfast, talking and laughing together. I had taken a small Christmas tree to put up in the rented house and Thomas, now twenty-one months old, sat in front of it, enthralled by the lights. We took him across the road to the beach for the morning, where he played with his new bucket making sandcastles, came back and had a late lunch of seafood and salad, followed by Christmas pudding, mince pies and ice-cream later in the evening. On Boxing Day, Sandra and David brought the girls over and they had a wonderful time playing with Thomas, treating him like one of their dolls. He thought it was great fun and was quite happy to fall in with whatever they dreamt up. I'd bought some cold sliced turkey and ham and more salad and made a pavlova for dessert. A perfect Australian Christmas.

During our two weeks with Thomas, he soon became comfortable with us again and was happy for us to take him to the beach without his parents, or for a drive in the car.

"You'll be home in time to help look after him during the terrible twos," Kelly joked, as she watched me

332

playing trains with him on the floor.

"Now that's something I can't miss!"

Unfortunately, our time with the family passed all too quickly. They had loved the hot weather and staying at the beach at Manly. We had taken many trips on the ferry to Circular Quay, as Thomas loved waving to the other boats we passed and Kelly and Andrea had enjoyed clothes shopping in the city.

As we waved them off at the departure lounge at the airport, I found myself looking forward to our return to London and spending more time together as a family. Mike had told me that he was looking for a contract in London so that we could remain in our London house. It would be nice to settle in one place, I thought. I had enjoyed my time back in Australia but now I was ready to live in London with my wonderful extended family.

As for mysteries, this time I was hanging up my hat for good.

Missing in Egypt

Anna Davies Mystery Series #1

A romantic travel mystery

Australian, Anna Davies, travels to Egypt with her lover to help him search for his brother, who disappeared whilst on holiday. The Valley of the Kings, Abu Simbel and the Temple of Karnak are amongst the settings for their search. Will they be able to track him down and find him alive - or is Ramy already dead? What tragedies await Anna and Kareem as they come closer to retracing his footsteps? This fast-paced action plot will keep you guessing until the end.

ISBN 9781478 257905

Amazon: http://www.amazon.com/ebook/dp/B007JOUIIE/

Large Print Edition:
http://www.amazon.com/ebook/dp/149121872X/

Smashwords:
http://www.smashwords.com/books/view/263417

Missing at Sea

Anna Davies Mystery Series #2

A romantic travel mystery

Three years on from Egypt, Anna Davies embarks on her first cruise with best friend Sandra. A few days into the holiday they are woken by three blasts from the ship's foghorn, indicating that someone has fallen overboard. A woman is lost at sea; the ship turns around to search for her, but she has disappeared into the night.

Was it suicide? Did she lose her balance and fall - or was there foul play involved? Did her husband push her? Would anyone be able to prove whether this was murder or an unfortunate accident?

What a perfect place to stage a murder!

ISBN 978-1542349055

Amazon: https://www.amazon.com/dp/B06XFKJTV4/

Large Print: https://www.amazon.com/dp/1544735111/

Smashwords:
https://www.smashwords.com/books/view/723008

Missing in London

Anna Davies Mystery Series #3

A crime mystery

Arthur Hambledon, Anna's best-selling author, has just finished his latest book which he says "will raise some eyebrows." Then Arthur disappears, along with the manuscript.

Anna Davies is working in London as a Senior Editor for a respected Publishing Company. When her most famous author goes missing, Anna is determined to find out what happened to him.

ISBN: 13: 978-1986740906

Amazon: https://www.amazon.com/dp/B07CYZTSZK/

Large Print edition:
https://www.amazon.com/dp/1718658842/

Smashwords:
https://www.smashwords.com/books/view/880026

Missing in France

Anna Davies Mystery Series #4

A crime mystery

When Mike accepts a two-year contract in France, Anna is delighted at the prospect of spending time in Paris and Marseille. She doesn't anticipate being drawn into yet another mystery, one which puts her own life in danger.

ISBN 13 9798 593280923

Amazon:
https://www.amazon.com/dp/B08X69SNJZ
Large Print:
https://www.amazon.com/dp/B08X63F2BN

Winston – A Horse's Tale

For horse lovers from teenagers upwards

Winston is a good-looking palomino horse whose life involves several different owners and many adventures. As you read his story, told by Winston himself, you will appreciate horse ownership from the horse's point of view. Born on a country property in Australia, Winston tells of his breaking-in and education and the different people he encounters – good, bad and ignorant. As well as his own story, Winston includes the experiences of other horses he meets along life's way.

Whether it's jumping, eventing, hunting or just hacking, Winston tries hard to please his rider. Follow his successes and his failures from his breaking-in to his show jumping win. It is an eventful life – the story of one Australian horse out of thousands, but one that you will remember!

ISBN 9781490368962

Amazon: http://www.amazon.com/dp/B00G9QOZGE

Smashwords:
https://www.smashwords.com/books/view/372140

Dangerous Associations

A crime mystery

An ex-husband, a new love, a stalker. Cathy Thompson's link to her ex-husband fills her life with threats and intimidation. She must either trap her stalker or find Geoffrey to put an end to her life of fear.

ISBN: 9 781501 062902

Amazon: http://www.amazon.com/dp/1501062905

Large Print Edition:
http://www.amazon.com/dp/1507554915/

Smashwords:
https://www.smashwords.com/books/view/493239

The Poinciana Tree

A crime mystery

This story is set around the beautiful Poinciana tree, with its amazing red flowers.

Suzanne Matthews arrives home from work to find the kitchen in disarray and her daughter missing. After searching the house, her eyes turn towards the garden, drawn to the Poinciana tree. Underneath its canopy she sees her daughter, slumped against its trunk.

When the police are unable to identify Jennifer's killer, they turn their attention to her husband, Mark. Whilst trying to cope with her grief, she finds herself fighting to prove her husband's innocence, as her world is turned upside down. She is inspired by another woman, who went with her husband to the Sudan as medical volunteers for a charity organisation.

A tale of raw emotion, desperation and acceptance.

ISBN: BO7X5R7KS1

Amazon: https://www.amazon.com/dp/B07XGGY2PZ

Large Print Edition:
https://www.amazon.com/dp/169438912X/

Smashwords:
https://www.smashwords.com/books/view/995821

About the Author

Rita lives with her husband on the Sunshine Coast in Queensland. When she's not writing or reading, she enjoys playing tennis, swimming and walking along some of Australia's most beautiful beaches.

You can learn more about Rita and her books on her website:

http://www.ritaleechapman.com

Reviews

Reviews are very important to authors. If you enjoyed this book, please consider leaving a review on Amazon.

Printed in Great Britain
by Amazon